DIFFERENT STROKES
Stories by Phil Andros & Co.

A Perineum Press Book
San Francisco

Cover drawing by Tom of Finland, © 1984.

Second printing, 1986.

Library of Congress cataloging in publication data:

Andros, Phil, 1949-
    Different strokes.

    "A Perineum Press book."
    Contents: The sergeant with the rose tattoo —
The economists — The house on the rue Erlanger — [etc.]
    1. Homosexuals, Male—Fiction. 1. Title.
PS3537.T479D5   1984   813'.54   83   83-18430
ISBN 0-912516-86-0 (pbk.)

Distributed by Subco, P.O. Box 10233, Eugene, OR 97440

DIFFERENT STROKES

For Ike & Jim
& the three bitches

Contents

NOTE

How does one describe a romantic encounter or a blowjob without naming it as such? Well, have a look at the early pre-Stonewall stories in this volume and you may find a way of suggesting it. The dark and secret world in which the American homosexual lived in the 1950s and 1960s had been illuminated only once, and that by Kinsey in 1948. In the literary world in those years, all of the authors had to conform to the only policy which publishers thought would sell their books: have the gay character commit suicide, or have his life end in disaster.

Magazine fiction was almost nonexistent. Occasionally a story with a theme differing from the heterosexual found its oblique way into print. Until 1952, when the magazine *One* first appeared in America, there was no viable periodical devoted exclusively to homosexual themes.

In Europe it was a little different. There in Zurich *Der Kreis* had begun to flourish in a slim bilingual publication in German and French, with an English section added in the 1950s. Those of us who were cajoled into writing for it (for no reward in francs, marks, or dollars) were very few indeed — some in America, some in Britain, so very few that each of us took several pen names for his work, to make the "Cause" seem more important.

In the course of my writing for *Der Kreis*, and later for *eos* and *amigo* in Copenhagen, I used about twelve different pseudonyms. Most of the first stories in this collection, with the exception of "The Biker," were written under the name of Ward Stames, an anagram of my own name. Here followeth some bibliographical data for those who are interested; if you are not, kindly skip this listing:

The tone of the early stories is different from that of the later ones. The policy of *Der Kreis* permitted only a lot of hand-holding, deep sighs filled with unrequited passion, fluttery sidelong glances, and not an erection to be seen or mentioned anywhere. The stories from *eos* and *amigo* were a little freer, but still without explicit sex. All we could hope for in those extremely closeted days was to influence the reader's imagination, and trust his gonads to do the rest. And what we produced was not pornography but erotica, one of the purest forms of entertainment because it has the most direct and immediate influence upon the body itself. A few of these stories might even be as effective as the wild ejaculatory shrieks of modern pulp characters [as they ejaculate]. At any rate, such tales as the ones here — if they did not satisfy *all* our yearnings in those dim dead days — at least helped to keep our vesicles emptied, our prostates churning, and our eyes looking for romance in the bulging basket we saw on that sailor coming down the street.

—Samuel M. Steward

DIFFERENT STROKES

The Sergeant with the Rose Tattoo

He was almost the first person in my little shop, for I had been officially open only three hours. He came tentatively to the door and stopped there, outlined against the lovely pale pearl of the Paris dusk, his face turned a little sidewise so that the red and green and yellow of my new neon sign made a kind of jewel around his head. His uniform was neatly pressed, the familiar drab khaki of the American Army, the three stripes of a sergeant's rank on his left sleeve.

I was more than astonished, for when you open a tattoo shop in Paris, somehow you think the first visitor will be a Parisian. How he ever found his way up the high hill of Montmartre to the dark little alley near the white dome of Sacré Coeur was almost a major mystery. I turned from putting up the last of my design cards and said, "Oui?"

In a dreadful halting pidgin French and English, he said, "Vous — you . . . er . . . ah remuer lez tattoos?"

In the smoothest French I could muster I said, "No, I regret it — you must go to a plastic surgeon for that; the whole cell structure must come out."

He looked so comically blank and woebegone that I had not the heart to deceive him any longer. "C'mon in, Mac," I said in English, "and take a load off your feet. You got a problem with a tattoo?"

His mouth opened slowly and then closed. "You — you're Ameri

1

can," he said. It was almost a gasp. It had a kind of heartache in it.

"I sure am," I said, "and you're the first customer." I turned to look at him more closely. I had been wrong in thinking that the last rays of the sun had somehow illumined my shop when he came in; instead, he brought light with him, in his golden close-cropped hair and the brilliance of his friendly smile. He was a distillate of all fraternity men and young football players and husky farm boys from the Midwest that I had left far behind—and I found myself opening to him, as I knew he opened to me—a compatriot in a foreign land.

"Holy cow," he said, "how'd you ever come to be working here in—in this place?"

"It's a long story," I said, and it was. I hardly knew how to tell it, nor that I even understood it myself. I remembered reading long ago somewhere in Gide that a man should make at least one decisive break in his life—with his family, his thought, or even the room in which he lived. And I had made two—one, when I gave up being music and drama critic for a San Francisco newspaper, and shocked my friends (most of whom could not survive the blow) by becoming a tattoo artist. But the second—and greater—separation came when I renounced my country—tired to the death of its phony optimism, its stifling puritanism, its bigotry—but most of all its hypocrisy, which in a kind of idiot dance-of-death publicly denied that it tolerated what nearly all of its citizens practiced on the sly. So I renounced its sham, rejected its money-grubbing, called it the only country which had ever passed from youth into decay without going through maturity—and left. My first papers of application for French citizenship were already circulating among the bureaus.

"Pull up a chair and sit down," I said, and he did. He moved with an easy grace, throwing one leg over the back so that he straddled the seat, and clasped his hands on the chair-back in front of him. I saw the crudely done letters above the lower knuckles of his fingers, but said nothing about them.

"You asked why I was here," I said. "Well, it was a case of my birthplace not coinciding with my spiritual home. I never liked America or its attitudes."

He thought about that for a moment. "I guess I don't know where my home is," he said. "I kinda think it's not in Germany, where I'm stationed."

"What are you doing there?" I asked.

"Military police," he said. He made a fist and rubbed it into his palm. "But I've been doing a lot of boxing for the company. Even some exhibitions. If I can get permission, I been thinking about doing some pro work around the German towns."

"I thought you might be an athlete of some kind." His shoulders were broad enough so that you had to turn your head slightly to see both of them, and his waist so narrow he could have swapped belts with a youngster. "What are you doing in Paris?"

"I got a week's leave," he said. "Another guy and I came over. He knew a babe here, and he's shackin' up with her."

"That kind of leaves you at loose ends, doesn't it?" I said.

"Yeah." He looked at the floor a moment, and then caught sight of his hands down between his legs, clasping the chair. "See?" he said, holding them out for my inspection. "I did that with a needle and some India ink. I wish to God I never had."

I had seen similar lettering before. On the fingers of one hand were the letters: L T F C; on the other—E S U K. When you put both hands together, palms down with the fingers interlaced, it spelled an obscene invitation. "That was a foolish thing to do," I said, but without reproach.

"Guess I thought it was funny at the time," he said ruefully. "Can you take 'em out?"

"I'm working on a method," I said, "but it's not ready yet. The only way now is sanding, or skin graft."

We talked for half an hour, a kind of nuzzling little conversation like two dogs sniffing each other to find out the extent of our friendliness. His name was Buck, and he came from Seattle, where a girl waited for him. Before he left, she had tried to use on him the oldest device to snare a man. "But I didn't quite believe she was gonna have a kid," he said. And now he rarely heard from her; either she had cooled, or he had—he didn't know which. His father and mother had separated. His mother was a tramp; he adored his father, but had lost him somewhere—a simple case of desertion when his old man had caught his mother in bed with a sailor.

A tattoo shop is usually a friendly place. The intimate nature of the operation stimulates confidences. In my long and battered career, I had seen thousands of young men, and with a bartender's patience heard their tales of joy and woe and defeat and triumph. But as I listened to Buck I was amazed at what was revealed. There were no

3

tough and artificial overlays of brutality and sophistication to be cut through; his very real purity lay close to the surface. Oh, he had been in bed with a few women—but somehow he seemed to have retained an attractive virgin quality. And like the romantic I am, and have always been, I began to project my own desires and idealizations upon the screen of his youth and charm.

He had a wonderful body; its beauty shone through the mustard-colored cloth. A few courses in life drawing years ago had taught me how to see through clothes. I noted that the definition of his muscles was superb; in the position in which he sat, the cloth was drawn taut across his magnificent thighs, and his calves were strong as the fabric tightened down to his well-polished army boots. His hands, big and well-shaped, a farmer's hands, lay quietly powerful as he talked, or moved a little to emphasize a point.

It has been said that no one ever asks another person to stay the night without having an ulterior motive in mind. But I can honestly say that such a thing was not in mine then, so it was with a heart nearly as clean as his that I asked him . . .

"Where are you staying?"

He gestured down the hill. "At a dump on the Rue Notre Dame de Lorette," he said. "I think maybe it's a—how you say it? *maison de passe.* Girls keep screamin' and runnin' up and down the hall, and drinkin', and people rent rooms but they're in 'em for only about thirty minutes."

I laughed. "And you trapped there in the whorehouse. I have an idea. How would you like to come stay in my apartment? There's an extra bed so . . . so you won't be bothered, and I—." But I need not have felt guilty. His face lit up, and his warm friendly grin was that of the long-lost returning home.

"Gee!" he exploded. "Wouldja mind? I'd like that a helluva lot. And say—" he leaned forward and laid one of his great hands on my knee. Mentally I shivered and almost moved, but I controlled my reaction. "—wouldja have any time to show me a little of Paris?"

If I haven't, I'll make it, I thought, and nodded. "As much as I can," I said, "and I'll steer you where to go for the rest."

"That's swell!" he said. His joy was touching, and his excitement grew. "Tell you what—I'll go down to that flophouse and get my gear, and bring it here, huh?"

"That's the best idea," I said.

4

He laughed in high glee, and sprang to his feet, knocking the chair over. He picked it up, smacked his fist into his palm, laughed again, and tilted his cap forward until the visor came down on his nose so far that I did not know how he could see underneath it. He almost pranced. "Gee!" he said again, grinning. "I'll get goin' right away. Now—now you wait for me. You won't go away, huh? You'll be here? For sure?"

"For sure," I laughed. His excitement was catching. "I'll be here."

And I watched him move out into the deepening night, jaunty, alert, handsome, trim. The streetlight picked out the spots of shine on his boots and belt. A few feet away he turned, gave me a half-salute and another grin, and then walked rapidly down the hill.

And thus began an odd and troubled week for me. I was disturbed in the first place because I had broken a cardinal rule: never mix business with pleasure. It might be hard to believe, but of the unnumbered thousands of young men who had passed under my needle, I had rarely overstepped the bounds. It was too dangerous, in a business sense. Among the young of a city, such a bit of gossip would flash like fire through a forest; and had any of them known my secret—well, I would have been popular, no doubt, but I would never again have made a cent in my business. Thus money kept me pure, as far as my clients were concerned; certainly the strangest thing that money ever did.

For the rest—well, I was no different from most of the brotherhood. Any handsome young man was a direct challenge. By cajolery, flattery, outrageous bribes, talk, the bait of records or books or pot or liquor, or money itself—I'd get him sooner or later. But what was Buck—customer or handsome young man? I refused to face the problem for a while.

That first night was both a pain and an ecstasy. We hailed a taxi when I closed the shop, and piled his gear inside. I directed the driver to pass by the Place de la Concorde, to show Buck the lights, and the great jewel box that was Paris by night. He laughed and hollered, and asked continually, "What's that building?" or said, "Look at that babe!" and pummeled me on the shoulder and back like an excited child. And when we reached the Rue des Saints-Pères, where I had an apartment formerly occupied by two fairly wealthy Americans, his enthusiasm overflowed.

"Gee, what a pad!" he exclaimed. "Have you read all those books?" He walked to the one wall where I had shelves to the ceiling. And then he peered through the door into the bedroom and saw the bath beyond. "And a real honest-to-god shower!" he said. "That's the first one I've ever seen in Europe, outside the barracks! Does it work?"

"It sure does," I said.

He started to unknot his tie. "I'm gonna take one," he said. "You mind?"

"Of course not," I said, "the place is yours."

He stripped off his shirt and then his T-shirt, and quickly stepped out of his trousers. And the room was filled with radiance. I had not been wrong in picturing his body—like a warm and living marble, sculptured by the hand of Praxiteles, descended from the Parthenon to grace my living room. As he turned his head, a great muscle on his neck flowed smoothly down into his excellent shoulders; the torso was flat and ridged, and the great ligament that held his belly swooped down like a birdflight into one side of his tight white shorts, and up the other, to vanish in the warm curve around his back. The torso of a faun—*Behold my beloved, he cometh leaping upon the mountains* . . . I turned to busy myself. My mouth was dry.

"I'll get you a towel," I managed to say, "and then I'll wash my face while you're in the shower."

He strode like a conqueror into the tiled cubicle, and a moment later I heard the rush of water. I shook my head, took a deep breath, and took off my own shirt. Then I got him a towel and went to the bathroom with it. I drew the water and washed my face, and then sat down in the bedroom until he finished. The April air was cool, but not unpleasant. From a corner of my window, I could look out at the lights along the Quai Voltaire and see the black shimmer of the Seine. The trees were misted over in the circles of light with the first faint green of their spring leaves.

The water stopped running in the bathroom. I heard the shower curtain being pushed aside, and the small soft sounds as he dried himself. And then he burst into the room like a blond panther, the towel wrapped around his middle.

"My gosh," he said, electrified. "What a beautiful tattoo!"

I looked down at the garland of roses and flowers that hung across my chest from each shoulder. "You like it?" I said, feeling foolish.

"I never saw anything like it!" he said with real enthusiasm. "Does

6

it go clear around the back?"

"Yes," I said. He put his hand on my shoulder and pulled it around to see. "Beautiful," he said. Then, "Gee, you're all goose bumps."

"Your hands are cold," I said, but it was not that. I stood up and put on a light dressing gown, and threw him a dark red one. "Be careful you don't split the back out of that with those shoulders," I said.

"I'll be careful," he smiled. "Don't worry."

Then we talked some more, and I poured him a glass of cognac, and at last we went to bed—he to his, and I to the twin beside him.

To judge from his breathing, he was asleep almost at once. But I lay for a long time listening to the night sounds of the city. The strong silhouette of his shoulder and back under the covers lay between me and the faint light of the window.

And I concluded, finally, that I'd rather have him as a friend . . . and then, partly at peace with myself, I fell asleep.

It was a wonderful week, but I neglected my business—a bad thing to do when one is just beginning in a new place. Together we did all the silly and wonderful things that tourists do, and the thrill was great for me. I was continually refreshed and stimulated as I saw Paris through his young eyes; it was almost like a first visit again, and once more I fell captive to the sweet grey spirit of the old city. We walked up the Champs Elysées, had apéritifs at little sidewalk cafés, and strolled through the Bois de Boulogne, marveling at the recurrent miracle of spring in Paris. I introduced him to the cafés of the St. Germain district, and we went once to the Folies Bergère. In the mornings the air was cool and sweet and thin as a golden sauterne, with little sparklings in it; the evenings were sometimes chill and yellow.

And I must confess, again, that the wall of my resolution lasted about three days; then it began to crumble from the repeated onslaughts of his beauty. His shyness disappeared, and whenever we got into the apartment, the first thing he did was take off his clothes. Not that I objected, of course; but the effect weakened me, to see him walking in his young glory nearly naked around the rooms, or play fully taking the boxer's crouch, or showing me a few karate moves over my protests. Contact with his body chilled and frightened me, for I saw the end of it that was hidden from him. And then gradually I began to say things, leading statements that he could hardly misin-

7

terpret — and he was not stupid.

I think it was the fifth evening. We had gone to bed, both mildly soused from a good deal of wine at dinner and cognacs afterwards at La Reine Blanche. The light was out. I was greatly depressed, and lay on my back in bed, aching with desire.

Suddenly he switched on the lamp between us and propped himself on his elbow. His handsome face was serious. He bit his lip a moment, and then said, "I'm sorry."

I stopped acting like a cheap theatrical ham and turned to face him. "Sorry for what?"

He flushed with embarrassment and looked down at his pillow, and punched it. "I—it's kinda hard to say. But—but I guess I know what's on your mind, these last few days . . ."

I said nothing.

"Well, the thing is, I just *can't*. The idea of it . . ."

"That's okay, Buck ole boy," I said. "I'll get over it." And then out of my frustration or spite or something like it, I added with some bitterness, "Besides, there'll be others coming along."

He looked at me for a long moment without speaking, and I saw the cornflower blue of his eyes turn frosty and darken. Then abruptly, without saying more, he switched out the light and turned on his side.

But by the next morning it was as if nothing unpleasant had happened at all. He had to leave the day after, so we made a celebration of the last twenty-four hours. We even went up the Eiffel Tower, over my loud complaints, for in all the years I had been going to Paris I had carefully avoided that excursion. Then in the afternoon, a lot of Pernod, and in the evening an excellent bouillabaisse. At the end of the meal, he leaned across the remains of our dinner and said, "I've got just one more favor to ask of you."

"Name it," I said through a happy haze.

"I want you to put a rose in the middle of my chest. Like in your garland. And someday I want the rest of it, too."

His request shocked me a little, and pleased me a lot. "You quite sure you want it?"

"I've thought a lot about it," he said. "Yeah, I want it. And too, that's one way I can be sure I won't ever forget this week." He toyed with a fishbone fallen to the tablecloth. "Or you," he added in a low voice.

8

So we got into a taxi and climbed back up the hill of Montmartre to the Rue Gabrielle, and opened up the shop. Then I went to the back room and got out the slanted bench. I put the screen up and did not turn on the shop lights—just those in my working area.

"Well, uncover the muscles," I said, and he took off his shirt. "And lie down." I put a pillow under his head and got my needles ready. Just before I started, I looked down at him stretched out on the bench, and said, "It's not too late to change your mind, you know."

He shook his head. "Nope. I want it. The big one just like yours." And then suddenly he put his arms up and clasped his big hands around the back of my head. He drew me down towards him, as startled as I had ever been in my life, and kissed me full on the mouth. Then he let go, and grinned up at me. "Now, go ahead," he said. "I just wanted you to know how I felt."

Trembling, shaken, I dipped the needle in the ink, and drew the first lines of the great scarlet rose upon the smooth swelling plateau of his chest.

It was a little over a year later, almost at the beginning of May. My shop had begun to prosper somewhat, and although I was not yet the rage of Paris, I had a good flow of customers. The number of women wanting tattoos surprised me, and to protect myself from the predatory females of Montmartre (and their vengeful *maquereaux*), I had bought a plain gold wedding ring, which helped to scare them off.

I still remembered Buck, of course, but in the deluge of young French *durs* and hoods, of sailors and soldiers, and in the making of new designs to satisfy their tastes, he had begun to recede into that opalescent realm of the past where we keep our best memories. My frustration had lost itself in a vague glow of pleasure that I always felt when I thought of him. He had written three letters to me, each enclosing some clippings. He had won bouts in his company and regiment, and the write-ups in the Army paper were flattering—"The Rose Boy-Cop," they called him. And then there were some clippings from German papers, and one victory picture of a referee holding Buck's hand high in the air, and he grinning broadly, with the rose plainly visible on his chest. When he went 'pro,' the crowds went wild over him; he turned out to be one of the most popular young boxers in Germany. And what was his name in Frankfurt and the other towns? Why, it was a natural: *Der Rosenkavalier!*

It was ten at night and I was getting ready to close. I heard my doorbell tinkle, and looked up. It was Buck. He had on slacks and a windbreaker, and was bareheaded; his golden hair shone in the light.

"Well, here I am," he said.

I played it low-key. "So I see," I said.

He came into the working area through the swinging gate, and sat down. "I'm outa the army."

"Really?" I said. "You're a pretty famous boy now."

He grinned in the old way. "Mostly your doing," he said. "That rose sure caught on. I guess you made me, all right."

The opening was there, and I said with a faint bitterness, "Hardly the way I intended, however."

He smiled briefly and then sobered, and moved his toe in a small circle on the floor. He said, without looking up, "I guess I've learned a lot in the last year. They always said travel was broadening. So what I'm really here for, in a way, is to apologize."

I felt a churning inside that formed into a tight knot, and then suddenly released. "No apologies needed, Buck ole boy," I said. "It's all in the past."

He looked up with his eyes, keeping his head down, and smiled. He said nothing.

"What's all this leading to?" I asked.

He stood up, raised his arms high in the air, and stretched like the handsome young animal he was, and looked down at me.

"To a final question," he said. "How's about putting me up for the night?" He lowered his arms, and put one hand on each of my shoulders. "We've got a lot to make up for," he said, and playfully cuffed me alongside the ear.

I looked at my ink-stained hands, lying in my lap. I had made myself a good life with them, and regained a measure of self-esteem. Why should one be at the mercy of the Bucks and Tonys and Chucks and Johnnys of this world? For me, there had been too much experience, it had multiplied itself until I was no longer under coercion from any person or thing. It was not my fault that it had taken this young man so long to learn, under how many faceless tutors I would never know. And it was not flattering to hear him now say something that I had known for many years, and had once told him was true. It would be so easy to show him the wedding ring, and tell him that I was married, and that my wife would not understand.

10

And yet, from the slowly moving column of young men that had passed before me in life, there were few that had come to join me, and call me friend; and fewer still who had offered me affection.

It took me less than three seconds to have these thoughts. Then I looked up and said, "Okay, Buck. I'm glad to see you back."

The Economists

He stood at the high French window, one hand holding back the deep garnet drape, and looked down the hill and across the bay. A flighty piping whisper of wind breathed in the night, and rustled the leaves on the trees in front of his house. Two flights down, the sidewalk glistened in the moisture from the evening's fog; and farther down the hill, over the yellow glow of the occasional street lamps and houses, he saw the black glitter of the bay, the patches of light that were the prison and the naval base, and the looping string of bright lights on the bridge that led across the water to the city on the other hill.

Then he heard the front door open and close, and a moment later he saw the husky figure of Danny, the street light on his head and broad shoulders. And at the point where the small sidewalk joined the main one, Danny turned around — as he always did — and gave a little half-salute with his hand to his bare head, back to the window — his little 'teacher-wave,' he had once called it, with his wry sardonic grin.

The professor waved back, and then let the drape fall, and with an absent motion pulled the cord that drew the folds together across the whole of the wall. Thus curtained in garnet, and carpeted in grey, with the few exquisite pieces of furniture gleaming expensively golden and mahogany in the subdued light, and the three walls of books showing through the arch into the library, the rooms became a dream of richness, a setting with some of the drama of a stage, for the tall and elegantly groomed figure of John Sanders.

12

He dug his hands into the pockets of his black and silver dressing grown, and sank into the deep chair beside the phonograph. He looked idly at the pictures on the walls—the sketch that Picasso had made of him when first they met at Gertrude Stein's, the framed signed photograph of André Gide that stood on the English desk, the excellently detailed Tchelitchev that hung on the right wall, and all the others, and he sighed.

It was a satisfactory structure of life that he had created for himself. At a comparatively early age, John Sanders was already a legend at the University—suave, intellectual, friend of the great and near great, winner of prizes and awards, author of three novels and innumerable articles, noted for the gemlike perfection of his every lecture, thoroughly the gentleman, always discreet—garnished with all the exotic blooms of a decaying civilization, and buffered against the unclean outer world by books and pictures and music, and his thoughts. At once friendly and yet curiously aloof, he never mixed with his colleagues, nor gave his students much encouragement.

There were very few persons who had ever succeeded in penetrating the wall around him, but Danilio was one; and fewer still who had ever seen him lose the dignity which cloaked him daily in his jampacked classes. He sighed again, and stretched his ankles before him and locked them like grey links, reaching out with one hand to the crystal bowl of the brandy glass. A little remained in the bottom; he swirled it slowly around, letting his hand warm the goblet, and the pleasant bitter fumes touched his nostrils. He sipped once—and the taste was like that of the *petite madeleine* for old Proust; its memory carried him back, back to Danny's first visit, and then earlier, to the time he first saw him . . .

Eight winters ago. He sat in the basement of the arts building, with the secretary of the Fine Arts Club.

"What's on the program tonight, Miss Carson?" he asked.

She fiddled with some papers on her lap. "Carl Preebe is going to show how all of Debussy's music is built on a small chromatic theme, Dr. Sanders," she said.

"Um-m. Very interesting," he said. And then he looked across the room. He had not seen the boy come in, but there he now sat—and suddenly the room focused upon him, the way the spiral of an Archimedes wheel draws the eye down into the center. He was not above

13

average height, but his body had the density to it that John Sanders liked. Upon the fine-shaped head the black hair lay tightly curled as on a classical statue; the jaw was square, and the chin deep-cleft. A hundred generations of northern Italians had lain together, and bred, to produce the boy's handsome Renaissance profile, full-lipped, straight-nosed with flaring sensitive wings. He was a 'white Italian,' without the tawny gold skin of the southerner, and his black hair quivered with a blue shadow of its own. He had crossed one knee over the other, and one large heavy hand, full-veined, lay quiet in its power upon his leg; the trouser had pulled up slightly, so that Dr. Sanders saw what looked to be the bottom edge of a tattoo upon his sturdy calf.

He nodded in the boy's direction. "Who's the newcomer, Miss Carson?" he asked.

She looked over the rim of her glasses. "Oh," she said, "that's Danny di Bella. He's just reentering this semester. He's been in the Navy four years. As a matter of fact, I think he's in your class in Victorian prose, Dr. Sanders."

"Ah, that might well be," murmured Dr. Sanders. "The class is so large I haven't seen to the back of the room yet. I must seat them alphabetically soon." And then, because he knew very well that Miss Carson did not know a word of Italian, he looked at the boy again, and said in a soft voice, "*Che bella cosa!*"

Miss Carson looked over her glasses again. "No, Dr. Sanders," she corrected gently. "It's Danny di Bella."

"Ah yes," he said, and smiled at her.

And sure enough, the great magic of the alphabet, applied to the vast lecture hall with its two hundred seats, brought Danny di Bella to view, and placed him in the third row from the front, directly under the view of the professor's dark green eyes. He became the central focus of the professor's voice and glance, just as a great handsome crewcut blond boy was the left side focus, and a handsome dark-haired lad the right center focus for his lecturing. Dr. Sanders never looked at the back of the room, which suffered from neglect.

More and more he came to talk directly to Danny, and to watch him as he lectured. It was extremely gratifying to see how alert his face was, a mirror to catch the polish of the exquisitely turned phrase, to reflect the glitter of a bon mot. And no matter how sly the innuendo, how esoteric the reference or subtle the double-entendre, he always caught the glimmer of comprehension from the young man's expression. The eyes danced, or the mouth quirked a bit at the corner in the quickly quenched beginning of a wry smile, or there was the ghost of a nod. And thus rewarded, Dr. Sanders reached towards new peaks of eloquence.His lectures crackled with wit and sensitivity. Once in a while, deliberately, he played with Danny to watch his reactions.

He remembered the lecture on *Sartor Resartus*, and Carlyle's philosophy of clothes. It had been—oh, so easy!—to slip into a small digression on the 'problem of the uniform.'

"It would seem then," he said carefully, "that the uniform of a military man—say, a sailor—is glamorous and perhaps romantic for a greater reason that that it is well-cut. It becomes a sort of psychic link to another world for us, a magic touchstone, a gazing glass or crystal ball in which we can see an existence which is far more appealing to us than the one in which we live."

He paused, noting the dull red burning of Danny's ears as the young man looked down into his notebook. And then with the timing for which he was known, and his delight at dropping the dreamy-eyed ones back to reality with a semantic shock, he said: "All this is merely hogwash, of course. The sailor is hardly braver or more romantic than a housewife plunging towards a bargain counter. Thus, ladies and gentlemen, the point that Carlyle makes—" and he was smoothly back on the track that he had left for Danny's benefit.

The boy was looking up at him, then, a slow and gently incredulous smile growing upon his face, an ever-so-slight negative shaking of the head as if in wonder, and astonishment. Their eyes caught and held a moment, and with a small but happy panic, Dr. Sanders knew that Danny knew.

But it was Danny who delivered the last jolt in the little episode. At the end of his brief paper on Carlyle, he put a single unrelated sentence: "Genet, in *Querelle de Brest*, says that the sailor's uniform was designed to decorate the coast of France rather than defend it."

And Dr. Sanders felt his own neck begin to burn.

During the few semesters remaining of Danny's education after the Navy interruption, they came to know each other as well as Dr. Sanders ever permitted a student to know him. There were occasional visits to the professor's office—'conferences,' technically, but really nothing more than good conversations, in which Dr. Sanders grew more and more to appreciate the quality of Danny's alert shy mind, honed to razor sharpness by youth and study and deep interest. Twice, Dr. Sanders took him to a concert across the bay; and once to the theatre. There were a few pleasant dinners together, always upon the neutral ground of a good restaurant. And Dr. Sanders could not remember at what point he stopped calling Danny "Mr. di Bella" in favor of his first name. But Danny always remained at his respectful student's distance, and never called him 'John.'

"Damn it!" John Sanders swore to himself one evening, after they had parted in front of a restaurant. It was a nasty little martyrdom that his life had forced upon him, a really ascetic existence, filled with delicate tortures that could have been devised by no lesser demon than Lucifer himself.

Take the particular hell of springtime, for example. For most people it was a season of delight, of filling the lungs with new fresh air, of walking hand in hand and being in love. For Dr. Sanders it was the season of torment. As the weather warmed, and jackets were left at home and shirt sleeves were turned up and collars opened at the neck, he watched the first faint tan begin to appear upon the arms and throats and faces of the young men before him. Out came the tight chino pants, the near-white bluejeans clutching the strong young thighs. Thin sweaters stretched across magnificent chests with downward pointing nipples—and Dr. John suffered.

And Danny—"Damned young devil! He knows what he's doing!" grated across John Sanders' mind, when he saw him on the first warm day—and yet he filled his eyes. Danny wore a thin sweater, evidently of nylon, stretched so tight that it was another skin—and of a red bright enough to blind the eye. The white of his forearms was still untanned and creamy, and his shoulders and pectorals swollen with power. As he turned his hand first one way and then the other, an excited pattern of muscles, small ones, flicked and flickered under his perfect skin. He wore black slacks, an echo of his midnight hair—and when John Sanders recovered from the near-physical blow of the sight of him, he began to blush, almost, at the quizzical line of Danny's half-smile turned upon him. That day the lecture came out with difficulty, for the flame burning in the third row dazzled his eyes. And somehow, from that moment on, Dr. Sanders

16

knew that there was no escape.

But he delayed the execution until nearly the end of the semester. And then Danny came to his office late one afternoon. The sun was lying golden across the desk and papers; the office smelled hot and stuffy and dusty. Danny sat in an office chair, one leg easily up over its arm. This afternoon he had on a white sweater, and by now his skin had claimed its heritage—the sun had left a lot of itself beneath, and Danny's color was a russet bronze in which his teeth flashed like a small ivory scimitar.

For a moment Dr. Sanders toyed with the notion of going for a swim with him, and then decided against it. There was the possibility of running into other students at the beaches or pools, and there was an even more subtle danger—the loss of dignity. He did not want to undress in front of a student, although he was obscurely ashamed of the necessity to maintain his aloofness. And Danny's body was so superb that his own must suffer, placed beside it. It was curiously difficult to maintain that vague 'superiority' or 'authority' with a body too thin, or too fat in the wrong places, or simply unclothed, or wearing trunks.

The professor looked at Danny, offering himself provocatively in the chair. "What do you say, fella," he said, looking at his watch. "It's four o'clock. How about a trip to the grocery, and then—my apartment for a steak and a salad? We can relax a little there. And come to think of it—you've not yet seen my apartment, have you?" He damned well knew he hadn't.

Danny swung his leg down from the chair arm. "No, I haven't," he said, with a carefully controlled enthusiasm. "And the steak sounds like a good idea to me."

Later, the dishes done and put away, they sat by the tall open windows, sipping benedictine and watching the evening dusk creep over the bay. The smoke from their cigarettes drifted slowly out into the purple air. The trees turned gradually black as the light faded, and the brilliant pinpoints of the city across the bay began to wink and sparkle. In the sky, the ashes of the splendor of rose and gold drifted slowly down behind the horizon. A Mozart concerto tinkled faintly on the phonograph.

"And what are you going to do, Danny, when you graduate?" he asked.

Danny motioned with his cigarette. "I honestly don't know, Doc. A job of some sort, I guess."

"Teaching?"

He could barely see Danny's wry grimace in the gloom. "Hardly," he said. "Not after the things I've heard from you about it. Although—" he went on, and hesitated a moment—"although if I thought I could ever bring to the profession the perfection that you have, I'd be tempted to go on to train for it."

"You flatter me."

"No, not really." The red point of the cigarette was almost all that Dr. Sanders could see—that, and the white sweater blurred into the deep chair. "You are the only one at this university—really, the only one—from whom I have ever got a thing. The rest—nothing but mediocrities, industrious or lazy according to their ambitions, but mediocrities just the same. Parrots, delivering word for word whole pages of textbooks as their own. Yours is the only thinking mind I have ever met while I've been here."

"Oh, Danny, that's nonsense. There are many good minds here, creative ones . . ."

Danny was obstinate. "Then I've not met 'em," he said from the dark. "But I've learned from you. You've taught me to think. You've taught me that a man can sit alone in his room, quietly, anywhere—and still engage in the most passionate activity in the world—thinking. You've done more than teach me to think—you've formed my mind and personality. You've given me what savoir-faire and sophistication I have. I've—I've inhaled you. I'll never have any thoughts from now on that won't be traceable—in some way—back to you and your classes."

"Danny, really—this is flattery beyond all reality."

"Please, Doc." He heard the desperateness in Danny's tone. "Don't interrupt me just yet, I've got to say it." He paused, and John Sanders heard him draw a deep ragged breath. Then he went on. "I've wanted to say these things to you for a long time, and I couldn't. If I don't say them now, I won't ever. And I wouldn't be able to now if it weren't dark."

In the silence, Dr. Sanders felt the thudding of his own heart. A premonition swept over him, at once heating and chilling him.

Danny went on. "I owe you a debt that could never be repaid in money. And if I tried to use another coin, I might offend you."

18

He was silent again for almost a minute. The Mozart came to a rippling end behind them, and the faint sounds of the water and the city rose from the darkness outside. A fresh smell of greenery crept in from the outer air. Against the lesser blackness of the opened window, the professor saw Danny stand up from the chair. He saw him put out his cigarette in the ashtray, and then watched the silhouette of his arms raise the white sweater slowly over his head, remove it, and throw it onto the chair. He heard the faint sound of the belt unbuckled, and saw the shadow step out of his trousers. And then Danny stood motionless, with folded arms, a darker body against the pale black of the night sky.

Finally he spoke. His words were hardly to be heard above the rushing blood in John Sanders' ears. "Please . . . please don't misunderstand me, Doc. I only hope the—the coin I offer is as genuine as the one I got from you." He laughed a little, low, nervous. "It's just returning oneself, after all—in gratitude, or tribute—to the one who did the work of creation."

In the tense magic of that moment, there flicked into the mind of John Sanders the picture of the clean-limbed Greek youths at Eleusis, offering themselves—soul and body—to the earth spirit, and the cold light issuing from the pit of wheat . . .

"Danny," he said, and could trust his voice no further.

From somewhere below them, in the vast blackness of the bay, a tugboat whistled twice.

John Sanders sighed again, and adjusted the folds of his black and silver dressing gown. It had been six years since that night, a long time. His own black hair had a threading of silver in it, a very little, at the temple.

There was a small grating sound of a key in the door, and he did not look up. Danny came in, and deposited a sack of things on the chair by the telephone. He took off his coat and hung it in the closet. And still John Sanders did not look up.

Danny walked to his chair, and rested easily on the arm of it. "Dreaming again?" he said. With the thumb and forefinger of his hand he kneaded the back of John's neck, and John made a little sound of pleasure, twisting his head.

"Just thinking," he said. "Where shall we go this summer? Scandinavia? Africa? Italy? France?"

"Anywhere you want," said Danny and took a small bite at his ear.

"They will play the full *Oresteia* in Sicily, at Syracuse in August, in the open air of the handsomest Greek theatre in all the world. Shall we be there?"

"Let's," said Danny.

The House on
the Rue Erlanger

It was only a single piece of notepaper this time, scrawled in his unreadable handwriting and his abominable French, but I managed to decipher it, for I had grown accustomed to it over the years. "When you come to Paris next week, don't stay at your nasty little hotel. Come stay with me on the Rue Erlanger. My nephew is here with me at the moment from Poland, but you can have the blue room. And then we can discuss at leisure the opening of the travel agency."

Just like him, of course. A European can smell American money clear across the Atlantic. I had made the mistake of telling him that I was at loose ends and looking for something to do. And he had already found a project—his project—for my little capital. Well, we would see about that. But I was surprised that he should invite me into the old house, for in all my travels to Europe, I could count fewer than a half dozen times when I had been invited into a private home.

And so it was that when I left the Aerogare at the Invalides, I gave the taxi driver the address of the old house. It was a dark November morning, and raining, and the old mood of a great enquiry cred and rose within me as we swept breakneck through the Place de la Concorde, with the cars hurtling by, and the street lights cutting daggers of light deep into the wet black asphalt of the streets.

I was lost on the west side of Paris, but the driver must have been

21

an honest man for it did not take us long, through tunnels garish with orange lights, past all the shops that looked so odd and unfamiliar, and on into the comparative quiet of Auteuil. The taxi stopped in front of the high iron fence, a solid black thing up to eye level, then branching into iron rods ending in pointed spikes. The house looked dark and foreboding; only a single light shone, high in the middle of the facade, an oval window like a Cyclop's eye directly under the roof—Prik's room.

His name had originally been Prikorszczewicz—which was too much for an Anglo-Saxon tongue to wrap itself around, so he had shortened it. The Americans whom he knew had a lot of fun with his abbreviated version. Just why he should have picked that spelling was a mystery, because he did know a little English. But Prik he chose, and Prik he was.

I paid the man and off he went into the dark channel of the street; then all was quiet. The rain dripped desolately from the near naked branches, and the sidewalk was thick with fallen leaves. I pushed the bell, frustrated, for I knew that he could not hear it on the third floor. I waved my arm above the solid part of the fence.

It must have been at least ten minutes, a long wet ten minutes, that I stood there vainly signaling. And then I saw a dark shadow in the window next to the lighted oval one and I waved again frantically. The bedroom light went on. A head looked out, and Prik gestured to show that he had seen me. Even at that distance of a hundred yards, I could make out the familiar white flattened napkin tied around his head, which he always wore while in the house. Asked about it, he would bristle, and say it was to keep his hair from falling into the cooking. But it was always soaked in salad oil, and the truth was that he had read somewhere in an old book of Polish folk remedies that it helped to prevent baldness. Several years of wearing it had not noticeably kept his hair from falling out; each year his widow's peak grew greyer and thinner, while the hair crept back on each side of it.

The light came on in the vestibule, and Prik hurried out to unlock the front gate, swearing in French at the 'dirty weather.' Instead of greeting me, the first thing he did was scold:

"If you had called me from the Aerogare as I told you to, you wouldn't have had to wait. I've been running to the window every two minutes for three hours."

22

"That's two hours before you knew I was due," I said. "And your two minutes are long—I stood there ten."

Prik gave a double flouncy shrug to both shoulders, like an irritated housewife in a cheap domestic drama. "You should certainly have called," he said. "Every two minutes for three hours."

Like some women, he had the faculty of not hearing what anyone said if it so suited his purpose, and most of his other thinking processes and reactions were feminine. This was odd, since he put such a high value on being a 'man' in all his appearances and actions, whether in bed or at a sidewalk café on the Champs Elysées. He was one who prided himself on doing only one thing to the young men he bedded with; and he boasted that he had never bowed his head, so to speak, in the worship of a handsome young man. And yet no one could camp louder or shriek more wildly than Prik when he was in the company of one of his goodlooking 'nephews' or 'cousins,' feeling euphoric and forgetting momentarily all about his vaunted maleness. And like most women who find themselves in the wrong, his favorite tactic was an aggressive counterattack on some minute facet of the argument then under way—a complete shifting of the subject, for he must win at all costs. Like all small-minded men, he would never admit he was wrong.

We hurried up past the circular gravel driveway in the faint light from the street lamp behind us, and into the lighted vestibule. It was the same lovely spacious place, with the red-carpeted stairway running up to the left, the glittering iron-encased cluster of lights hanging down from the high ceiling, the elaborate coat-of-arms of the Comte and Comtesse de Lukler set into the mosaic floor. But the odor of must and mildew was overpowering; the air was chill and damp.

Here in this ancient house Prik had lived for fifteen years. The Luklers had long ago retired on their profits from making ice cream to live in an even more sumptuous château in Switzerland, but he—their good friend—had stayed on here as a kind of unsalaried guardian of the place, having closed off the first and second floors, and retired to the third where he had a small bedroom and a living room, and where there were—if I remembered correctly—two other huge bedrooms, one with red carpeting and figured cloth on the walls and bed, and the other one with blue. There was also a bathroom where Prik not only made his toilette, but used the washbowl as a sink. A small kitchen stove had been installed in one corner. It was a makeshift arrangement, but he had grown used to it. As for me, I always felt that there was something vaguely wrong either about washing oneself or the dishes in the same basin. But that was French for you, or Polish — or just ordinary European.

We climbed to the top of the stairs, puffing. Prik had grabbed the little lightweight case that I took on the plane with me, leaving me to lug the big heavy one to the top. He ran ahead, snapping lights on and off, illuminating our progress by pushing the *minutières*, those practical light switches invented by the frugal French to make sure that one did not waste electricity; they remained on for one minute and then went off. And he was busy unlocking doors as we went through, and relocking them behind us.

It was no warmer in his living room. There was a kind of indefinable tomb-coldness to the place; it seemed like a house out of a Poe story — the house of Usher, perhaps — and the dampness stank as must have the underground corridor — wet with dripping water and crusted with lime — down which Montresor led Fortunato towards the lure of the cask of amontillado. The air was soaked with damp; you felt it in the wandering little currents of air our progress stirred up, and my hand — resting for a moment on one of the ancient velvet cushions of the sofa — rose involuntarily at the sensation of cold and wetness, as though I had brushed against a night animal in a dark wet wood.

Prik snapped on the glaring overhead light and set my small bag on the floor. He looked at me critically.

"You are a lot older," he said. It stung me.

"Neither of us is twenty any more," I said.

That set him off. He started one of his orations, waving his hands. "But we can be!" he said excitedly. "We can think young and dress young and act young — and that makes us young!"

"It makes us look like vain old aunties," I said, "and after all, it makes no difference any more. The young no longer do more than let their eyes pass over us. We never reach their consciousness; it's as if they looked at a post or door or a chair."

"Not at all true," Prik began.

I sighed. I did not feel like a discussion about being a thing of beauty and a boy forever just at that moment. "Later," I said. "Prik, please, later. I'm terribly tired now."

He paused and stared at me for a moment, and then his slackened

24

jowls fell into the semblance of a grin. "Of course," he said. "I forget." He picked up a suitcase—the big one this time—and started towards the bedroom door. With his hand on the latch, he paused and spoke in English. "My nephew, he is in there. He is sleeping. Do not speak to him now. He has been crying. The other door is not unlocked yet. We must go through this way."

I was startled. "Crying?" I said. "What for? How old is he?" for all of Prik's 'nephews' were always between eighteen and twenty-four, his topmost limit, and I had a picture of a tousle-haired child of eight holding a teddy bear, or the French equivalent of one.

Prik shrugged. "Twenty-two. And he is crying because I scolded him."

"Why?" I asked, intensely curious.

He shrugged again. The door was already open and he quieted me with a movement of his lips. We walked past the bed. A small night light was burning in the diagonal corner of the room. And in the rumpled covers of the red-upholstered bed, I had a brief and shadowed glimpse of the large frame of a young giant, silver-haired and blond as only Poles and Danes can be, strong and clean-necked, his face turned towards the wall. His right shoulder and arm and the white strap of his undershirt were above the cover. I unconsciously drew in my breath—the form of the shoulder was so muscular and strong, and the skin so white with ruddy undershadows—all 'milk and blood,' as the Germans say—that it was like seeing a jewel in a hen's nest; utterly foreign to its environment, completely incongruous and out of place. The shoulder and head were classical; they belonged in sunlight on a piece of statuary, not in a bed in a faded room with crumbling draperies, in a dank and dismal house on a rainy November evening in Paris.

I paused, looking at the beauty of that fragment of his body, and then I saw Prik motion me onwards to the door to the blue room, which he was holding open.

The room was as spacious as the red one, but the color of it—blue carpet, blue-grey paper on the walls, a mirror with a black and ruined surface hanging at one side, and plaster scaling from every corner of the ceiling, the fragile spindly furniture, beautiful as it was—all these things made it seem colder than ever. I shivered. "I'm freezing," I said.

Prik tossed that one off easily. "I'll make a fire tomorrow morning," he said. "There is almost no coal to be had in Paris. We must be careful with what is left."

I grimaced a little, since his back was turned. It was the same old Prik—always the penny pincher save when it came to spending money on something he wanted. I might as well make the best of it.

"Are you hungry?" he asked. "Have you had anything to eat? I don't have much—"

I made a gesture with my hand. His inflection told me what I was to say. "I don't want a thing, *copain*," I said. "Had a big meal on the plane. Actually, Prik, I am so tired I think I'll go right to bed if you don't mind."

Prik was obviously relieved. "I'll see you in the morning then," he said, and carefully closed the door to the red room. I heard the lock click, and knew that I could not poach that night, but must use the other door and the extra toilet. Ah, well, there were twenty nights to go . . .

I undressed hastily, and steeling myself with a shudder, slipped my naked legs down into the cold damp sheets of the old blue bed. It soon warmed up, though the feeling of wetness remained. I lay looking at the ceiling, and the spell of the quiet house grew stronger on me. There was absolutely no sound anywhere; if there had been noise on the Rue Erlanger, it would never have reached beyond those silent walls and the labyrinth of doors and passages that cut off all sound.

Once in my travels I stole a piece of the mosaic floor from the baths of Caracalla in Rome, and I am so made that by simply holding that stone in my hands and closing my eyes, I could become the floor from which it was taken. I could feel the young naked Roman feet slipping and sliding over my warm hot surface, and hear the tense and rapid Latin; sense the water from the baths flowing over me—feel the steam curling above me, and the hot juices of excited young men pouring into the mortar around me. So now, reaching up to touch the faded rough tapestry with which the bedframe was covered, and shutting my eyes, I felt the room peopled with the uncounted dozens of Prik's young men—naked, advancing, retreating, whispering, smiling, scowling, reaching out to touch me, bending to embrace me, or kneeling above my head—some stern, some pleading or begging, some commanding, all of them rampant and excited, hairy-legged or smooth, blond as sunlit gods, or dark with the tawniness of Italian suns, the Arab boys with flashing eyes, the crew-cut American soldiers gleaming with ruddy health, the champion skiers with muscled thighs, the swimmers with arms gleaming as they cut the dark water . . .

The room was full of dreams, and all night the bed was warm and snug.

The next three days were somewhat hectic, until Prik could make up his mind to accept this invasion of privacy that I seemed to be for him. He nagged at me like a shrew, for everything under the sun. He objected to the way I shined my shoes—me, who had been in the Navy for six years and could apply a spit-shine along with the best of them! He scolded me for not scraping the butter off the roll with my knife, but cutting it instead, so that I got a small piece of foil with it and swallowed it—"A mortal poison!" he yelled. He gave me lessons three times over in how to lock and unlock the doors and gates, and cautioned me innumerable times about leaving the lights on. He insisted I wound the cuckoo clock wrong, complained that I smoked too much (a pack a day against his three litres of wine), bought Polish bread until I went out to get the French *baguettes* myself, and withheld an extra set of keys from me until I was on the point of moving to a hotel. In short, he acted like a crotchety old maid, seeming almost jealous of the house and its contents, which in a very real sense were not his, nor had ever been. Besides these annoyances, I saw also that the fountain of ideas in him had long since dried up, leaving only a crust of opinions. And his once open mind—like a fatally wounded oyster—slowly closed its shell so that it might perish undisturbed.

In those three days I never even met Erik, the 'nephew.' The boy got up at some ungodly hour, donned his worker's blues, and went off at six in the morning. This uncivilized schedule put him back at the house a good three hours before Prik himself got home from his office, but on each of those days I was even later in returning, and each time Erik had already gone to bed.

The curiosity I felt over why he had been crying still burned strong within me. I kept at Prik about it until he said, with some annoyance,

"I was scolding him because he was acting like a woman."

"In what way?" I asked, and then prodded him again. "I thought that was the way you treated him anyway, once you got him in bed."

That really annoyed him. "Well, this time he was on his knees

27

and had his arms around my legs, and was really acting like a dirty —" and he used an obscenity that was very misogynous.

"But why was he crying, in heaven's name?" I persisted. Prik looked uncomfortable and then tossed his head, so that he shook the raddles of loose flesh under his chin.

"Oh, he said that I was treating him like a whore, that I never helped him to enjoy himself while I was screwing him, that I ordered him around too much, that I kept him from meeting any girls because he doesn't speak much French, and lots of other things." He moved his shoulders angrily.

"All true?" I asked. Prik changed the subject. "Bring me the lettuce," he said. "What else do you want in the salad tonight?"

After that I decided that if I wanted anything done I would have to do it myself. Accordingly, I was in the house at four o'clock the next afternoon when Erik came home. I was lying on the bed in my dressing gown reading, and I had with foresight left open the connecting door between my room and his. I heard the hollow echo of the slam of the great front door, and then the sound of him coming up the stairs, and finally I heard him turn the latch of his room and enter. That was my cue.

I got up and went to the door, book in hand. The room was fairly light, for the shutters were open. I had set myself to see a handsome young man, and I was not disappointed. His hair tumbled from the little blue worker's cap like a curling golden waterfall arrested in motion. His shoulders were broad, and stretched the pale denim of the worker's jacket tight to bursting across his wide chest. Through the close-fitting blue trousers I saw the muscular thighs at work as he took two steps into the room, the great bulge at his crotch. And then he saw me and smiled, and walked towards me with his hand out. "I . . . am . . . Erik," he said in French, somewhat haltingly. Then he said it again in English, and startled me.

I answered him in English, "I suppose you know who I am," I said. He grasped my hand in his big one, twice as large as my own, with a broad strong back to it on which two prominent veins, I noted with some detachment, roughly formed a reversed letter R. "I am surprised to hear you know English."

He grinned even wider, with a dazzling effect of white teeth. "Do not, please, tell . . . to Prik. I learn . . . it from American girl. She is . . . daughter? of American colonel here . . . Paris." He looked down, fiddling with his cap, and then threw it suddenly on a chair. "Perhaps . . . I get married," he said, suddenly scowling. "Leave . . . all this," and he gestured widely at the room. Then he looked at me in alarm. "Do not . . . tell?" he said.

"You can be sure I won't," I said.

He smiled down at me. He was at least seven inches taller than I. I looked at the full red coloring of his lips the high cheekbones, and the strong square Slavic jaw. I felt an unreasoning panic. This stalwart young man was hardly acting with what Prik described as the actions of a woman. Then suddenly he completely astounded me. We were standing fairly close; he took one step, and I felt his arm around my shoulder. With his free hand he tilted my chin up, and kissed me full on the mouth. I felt a little flick of his tongue across my lips as he opened his mouth slightly, and then he released me and stood back, smiling. My heart was pounding.

"I . . . believe now . . . I *sure* you won't tell," and he threw back his head and laughed. Then he said, his whole manner changing a little, subtly, "Now . . . you excuse? I must—" he gestured—"make the *toilette*—how you say? Wash . . . up?"

"Y-yes," I stuttered. I pulled the cord on my dressing gown tighter, and stumbled towards the door of my room. I looked back at him; he was already stepping out of his pale blue trousers, and I saw his golden thighs . . . and then panting, sweating, and half dizzy, I went into my room and shut the door behind me, leaning against it.

I had perhaps ten minutes to make up my mind. He was not drawing the bath water, but I heard splashing. All too vividly I imagined him giving himself a 'little French bath'—rubbing the washcloth over his magnificent arms and chest, raising his arms, scrubbing violently, and then his white torso—and first one foot, and then the other, raised high and put into the bowl. I walked around the room, sweating. And then I decided: to hell with Prik, and come what may.

I opened the door to Erik's room again. I closed the shutters and turned on the faint night light, far on the other side of the room. Then I pulled down the covers of his bed part way, threw my dressing gown on top of his work-clothes, and crawled in. I was shivering, and not from the dampness this time, for I did not even notice it.

Three minutes later I heard him come into the room. He could not see me, for the head of the bed was high and I had moved into the darkest corner. But he must have immediately noticed the shutters closed, and the small light turned on. He walked naked across the room, easily, to his clothes, still not turning to look at the bed, and fumbled in his jacket pocket. My dressing gown lay on top of it; he moved it aside. He took out a package of cigarettes and lighted one. And then still without turning, he said over his shoulder,

"You . . . want . . . cigarette?"

"L-later," I said in a strangled voice. "I want . . . you." The magnificent white body, poised with legs apart slightly, the hollows in his strong buttocks shadowed in the light, turned. He laughed and came to sit on the side of the bed. I reached up to touch the warm and soap-fragrant skin of his broad chest. Then he carefully crushed out the cigarette and leaned over me, staring intently out of clear eyes. Slowly his face descended, and I found myself drowning in the pools of blue.

His mouth opened, the curve of his lips magnified (so close!) that it seemed like a drawn bow. His teeth parted and his tongue found my half-opened lips, and entered. Against my belly I felt the hard column of his cock, pushing, thrusting, so strongly that I felt he might be trying to enter where there was no opening.

There were no covers left on the bed when we finished an hour later. How many times he had come — and I had — neither of us had counted, nor how many times he had screwed me. His giant's body lay finally quiet, save for the still deep breathing that gradually slowed; and we were both wet with sweat.

There was no question in my mind that Erik had got even with Prik for most of the treatment that he had endured. His manhood had been established once again, and he had given me a new center of consciousness.

Suddenly the old bleak house became for me the most pleasant of places, as for the next week the new pattern of my life continued. The blue room seemed not half so cold and chill, and the red room — well, that was a warm and agreeable refuge against the rains of Paris, which beat violently across the shutters but could not extinguish nor cool the new heat in me. And each day, afterwards, Erik would rise and dress and disappear into the great mouth of Paris before Prik got home.

I could see Prik growing increasingly irritable, and was mildly amused. He complained once that Erik was always out, and that he had not come to Prik's room for a long time.

"He does not know anyone in Paris," he fussed. "Where can he go? What can he be doing?"

"Probably just out having a drink at a nearby bar," I said, "and playing the American pinball machines."

And then I came home late one evening myself, to find Prik staring at an opened pneumatique which he held in his hand. He swore in Polish when I came in, and got up to open a table drawer. He was muttering all the time I was taking off my raincoat.

"What's the matter?" I said. I turned to watch him. He was gluing the flap of the special delivery letter back on the envelope. He faced me, and his expression of fury had drained his face of all color. He threw the pneumatique down viciously.

"The dirty . . . pig!" he exploded.

"Who?" I asked innocently.

"A girl," he said with hatred in his voice. "A dirty American tramp. Erik knows her, somehow. She wrote to ask him to come to see her tonight."

"You opened the letter?" I said evenly.

"Of course!" he said angrily. "Why not? I bring that boy here from Poland, I treat him good and buy him food and clothes — and he goes off with a dirty —con who . . ." The rest was vile.

I kept silent. The truth was indeed different. Prik had made of the boy practically a slave, had guarded him jealously for himself, and refused him all the freedoms. I went to my room and went to bed — and it was only much later that I heard him and Erik in a violent argument. At the head of my bed was a speaking tube, leading to Prik's bedroom, through which the old Comtesse de Lukler had formerly summoned the maid from her quarters. The sound of the quarrel came clearly through the tube. Unfortunately, it was all in Polish and I could not understand a word of it. But the violence of it even rattled the metal of the tube. I finally closed the shutter over the open end in my room, but I could still hear the voices. And then there was a great slamming of doors, and I heard Erik undressing. Was I mistaken, or did I once catch a great dry sob from him? It was hardly the night to go to comfort him.

And it was almost impossible to live with Prik for the next two days. Again I thought seriously of moving out to a hotel, but that would mean not seeing Erik again, and we were really getting along very well. He told me of the argument, and how Prik had found out about the girl.

"Take it easy," I said. "Just go ahead and marry her. You're not really one of us anyway; you're just a healthy sexual animal."

Erik turned and smiled across the pillow at me. "You . . . understand," he said, and he reached over to grab my shoulder with his big hand, and dig his fingers in. "I like . . . you . . ."

I stroked his thigh.

But things could not rest like that. Prik was sullen and silent for a while, and then one evening he had a visitor—a man in a belted black French version of a British trenchcoat. I heard Prik go downstairs to let him in, and peeked at them as they came up the stairs. And then with only a little shame on my part, I opened the shutter of the speaking tube. This time it was all in French.

I listened with growing alarm. The man was evidently a good friend of Prik's—they used the 'tu' form of speech with each other. I gathered that the visitor was a private detective associated with some agency.

"—but the girl will not know that," Prik was saying. "You can give her a brief glimpse of your badge, she will not know the difference, and tell her you are from the police. And then be very polite—just ask her a few questions. Ask her how long she has known Erik Trycznski, if he ever mentioned having a police record, when he came from Poland, if he has ever spoken of any Communist affiliations, if he has ever tried to talk about American military plans or get her to ask her father anything—you know how to do it. Do not make any—" there I missed a word or two— "but just frighten her. You understand?"

"Yes, I understand," the man said.

"All right," Prik's voice went on. "And here is something for your trouble. You will bring me a full report, yes? And you will go see her tomorrow? So, here is her name and address—Patricia Turner—you can read it? 28 Boulevard Victor-Hugo, Neuilly . . ."

Automatically, I don't know why, my hand sought a pencil and I too wrote down the name and address. Then I lay back thinking.

It was really a very clever plan, and there was absolutely nothing I could do about it. The phony policeman would visit Patricia Turner and question her; she would get frightened, for after all she had not known Erik long, and probably knew nothing of his background, or very little. She would feel her father might be compromised in whatever military position he held in Paris. There would be a letter written, and she would tell Erik she was going back to America or something like that. Perhaps she would even actually go. And I could not tell Erik, for Prik would immediately learn — and I did not want that open a break between him and me . . .

The letter arrived two days later. I saw the postman thrust it through the slot in the iron fence. It fell into the glass-backed letter box, and I went downstairs to check. It was addressed to Erik. I went back upstairs and dressed and left the house. I did not trust myself to be there when Erik got it. And so I had dinner alone that night in a quiet place on the Rue Helder, and got home late, nearly midnight. There was no sound from Prik's room, and I looked cautiously into Erik's. His bed was empty. I went to bed, saddened. That trap had been sprung, the gate had shut. Erik's chances for escape now seemed very remote indeed. The original pattern had been reestablished, and behind Prik's closed door a young man had fallen back into the pit . . .

Ah, well, it was too bad — but it was really not my affair. I had one more day in Paris before going back to the States. There was a lot of last-minute shopping to do. And it was at the perfume counter of the Galéries Lafayette that the idea burst upon me.

That evening I wrote a little letter. It was addressed to 'Mlle Patricia Turner' and sent to the Neuilly address in the suburbs. It said:

Dear Miss Turner,

The man you thought was a Paris policeman was only a private detective. He was hired by a homosexual who is in love with Erik. The purpose was to frighten you away from Erik, because the man who hired the detective is jealous of you. He feels that he may lose Erik to you.

Erik is a perfectly respectable young man. He is not a spy, a criminal, nor a Communist. And he is not a homosexual, unless you make him one by abandoning him.

Please do not tell Erik how you found this out. He would

33

know at once who tried to help. I hope you will marry him
and be very happy together.

I did not sign the letter. I mailed it at the Aerogare before I took the
bus to Orly airport. I justified myself by remembering that I once
was a Boy Scout, and we were always committed to do one good
deed a day. I felt, as the letter dropped into the box, that this one
might be valid for a whole year's requirements.

The Biker

I guess I'm what some people would call a tough guy. I don't exactly know why they do. Something about the way I look, I reckon—or kinda tighten up my eyes when I talk. Mebbe it's a kind of reputation I already got—some guys pass me on to others, if you know what I mean. There was a pansy in Kansas City who said afterwards he'd been scared to death pickin me up, accounta the sideburns scared him. And there was a boot-queen in San Francisco—you know, one of them queers likes to have you rub your boots in their faces and make 'em go down on you—who said he thought I was tough accounta the way I wore my motorcycle cap.

Anyways, why it is I don't know, but traipsin around over these here United States, I sure been able to get what I wanted everyplace I been. Cunts, sure—plenty of 'em, I affect 'em just like I do the fruits. But after bein on the road, and a coupla years in San Quentin for a bum rap I don't get so much kick anymore outa cunts—they're too damn loose. They get so hot with me suckin their tits or eatin their pussies a little that they come 'fore I'm anyways near ready. In San Quent I had me a coupla gobblers, damn cute kids—one of 'em knew more tricks with his mouth than any bitch I ever ran into. Christ! It was wonderful! He'd run his tongue round the end of my cock, or he'd make it kinda quiver on the head of it, or he'd take it clear back in his throat until you could feel it begin to go down. That'd set me wild and I'd grab his head and push him down on it till he'd gag. Once I pushed too hard and tore that there skin at the back of his throat. Goddamn, he sure looked sick! But the next week when he was outa sick bay he was right back askin for more of my old eight inches.

Yeah, that's what I got. Not much more'n parlor size, huh? But I kin do more tricks with it than forty feet of grapevine. Sure, Mac . . . you can buy me a drink—bourbon, straight. Yeah, I was in the Navy for a while, too. You guessed it from my sayin sick bay, huh? You were, too? Well, my name's Jack. I'm six-two, one-ninety, and my hair 'n teeth are my own. Twenty-eight, free, white, and single. I just got in town this afternoon.

Well, I hadda *lot* of adventures on the way. All kinds—whadyuh want—men, women, or animals? Sure—sheep. I don't mind stickin it in a nice clean sheep—only you gotta watch out or they'll shit all over you. A man? Christ, yes—I had a dozen on the way from St. Louis.

Well, there was that kid I met in Kansas, f'rinstance. It was about three weeks ago, middle of August, and I was high-tailin it along the highway—goggles on and all—and had made about 350 miles that day, counta I got a late start. Got tight in St. Louey and didn't get up till noon. Well, my old ass was gettin tired, and ridin there in Kansas is sure monotonous with them long straight roads goin off in the distance far as you can see. The wind kept me pretty well cooled off, but I was kinda itchy—you know how it is. Us wheelers calls it road-burn—your old cock gets all knotted up and hard from all dat ridin, and Christ, you think you're gonna go nuts. I'da liked to a had a good blowjob right there, and I'd had that damn road-burn all afternoon, my old John a-laying there on the cycle seat, tensin up and sorta raisin his head to look around— you know what I mean? By God, it sure is wonderful how they seem to got a life of their own, ain't it?

Well, I'd been keepin my eye peeled on the fields a-looking for a calf, even though it ain't exactly the season of the year for them— and I'd seen a storm a-coming up from the south. I sorta figgered I'd have about a half hour more afore it hit me, and I'd oughta been able to find a place to run in in that time. But I reckon I miskalkelated, cause after about ten minutes I felt a coupla drops, and jesus, there wasn't no shelter in sight nowheres. I was just beginnin to goddamn it, when I rounds a buncha trees (only ones I'd seen for miles) and there standin right by the roadside was a farm kid with his thumb up hitchin a ride. I don't generally like to give rides, cause usually it's too much chance to take on balancin—and if a guy ain't never rode a wheel afore he's likely to throw you off when you're hittin a curve or doin eighty. Man, that's fatal. So generally I don't stop, but this time I did because I thought maybe duh kid knew someplace wheres we could go to get outa the rain, cause the drops was gettin bigger.

So I pulled up beside him.

"Hi!" he says. "Gimme a lift?"

"You know howta balance?" I asks.

"Sure," he says. "I rode one of them things lots."

"Anyplace to get outa the rain?" I asks.

"Yup," he says, " 'bout a mile down on the Stafford farm. Old man Stafford's got him a storage barn about two miles from his farmhouse, but we can get in it on account I know now."

"Okay," I says, "hop on."

He was a good-lookin kid, about two inches shortern me, about six feet, and he had blond curly hair and a good tan. I kinda envied him that on account my goggles leave white circles around my eyes. All he had on was one of them combination overalls with a bib up front, you know, the kind with straps over the shoulders, and he was built like a brick shithouse, no kiddin. I thought I had a good build but this was better. And them coveralls fit him like a glove. I felt ole Betsy begin to move about in my pants when I looked at that cute little ass of his—bet he was tight as anything, and I could just see me sorta partin the cheeks of it like as if it was cabbage and sockin my old dong right down to the heart of it. I could see from the front he had quite a piece a baloney himself, big bulge down there atween his legs.

He hopped on and then he stopped a minute. "What're you waitin for?" I growls. "Grab aholt of me, around me, and lets get goin—it's gonna rain like hell in a minute!"

He pressed close to me and then he kinda put his arms around my middle like as if he was half afraid to, and I remembered I had my shirt open clear down to my bellybutton and he'd have to touch my hairy chest and belly. "Fer Chrissake," I says, "a little hair ain't gonna hurt you—grab aholt tight." With that he did, and those big forearms crossed in front of me and held tight. The kid smelled like hay—kinda fresh and . . . good . . . and we lit out for the barn.

37

Not soon enough, though. 'Bout a half mile from it, the rain began to come down in buckets. I was afraid the damned motor would flood on me, it was that bad. I kept holdin her down, and I could hear the kid kinda gaspin behind me because he din't have no goggles and he was half blind with the rain. Finally he yells in my ear, "There she is!" and I rattled up to the barn door, skiddin the gravel in a hailstorm up agin the wood. He jumped off and ran around the corner, and in lessn a minnit he opened the door from the inside. I wheeled the bike in outa the rain.

The both of us was soaked to the skin. The water was runnin outa my jeans and would of got into my boots ifn I'da had 'em tucked down in the way I usually ride. The kid was kinda laughin and tryin to get the hair outa his eyes, and his overalls was soaked clean through except for a big dry spot right on his front where he'd been huggin me close from behind.

"Looks like we gotta dry these things out," I says.

"How?" he says. "They ain't gonna be any sun till tomorrow, and we can't light a fire in here."

"Okay," I says, "looks like we're stuck here for the night or until it stops rainin."

"Yeah, I guess so," he says. He looks kinda worried. "What'll my folks say?"

" 'Bout what?" I says kinda sarcastic. "Spendin the night with a strange man in a barn?"

He turned red as fire. "Naw," he says. "They jest might worry." He began to unbuckle his shoulder straps, and then he started to peel off his overalls. Peel's the word for it. Being wet made them tighter, but he managed to get 'em off. Meanwhile I'd took off my jeans, soppin wet, and hung 'em up, but I left my cap and boots on. He was standin with one foot up on a box and tryin to wipe the water off him with his hands, and shiverin a little. He kept his back turned to me, bashful-like, but that was okay, that was the part I liked lookin at. Jesus, it was a good back—and real muscled legs, but mostly I liked that tight little ass. It looked hard as rock. And I could just see me spreadin the cheeks apart with my hands like you'd open an oyster and gettin in there where it was nice and hot. Thinkin like that made be begin to get hard, and so to stop it and not to scare him to death I opened my kit and pulled out a towel and flung it to him.

"There," I says. "Wipe."

"Gee, thanks," he says. He took it and wiped his hair and then gave himself a good rubdown with it. But he still kept sorta turned away from me as if he was bashful about showin his cock. I pulled a pint of likker outa the bag and took a good stiff snort of it. Then I says, when I got my breath back, "What's yer name, kid? Can't spend the night here without we interduce ourselves. Mine's Jack." I stuck out my hand. He had to turn around on that, and I looked down at his cock.

"Ed," he says, "Ed Johnson." Then he saw where I was lookin and he kinda made to cover it up, but then he musta thought that was silly because he took the towel away. I still had the bottle in my hand. "Drink?" I said, and grinned at him. That grin had knocked more cunts over than you'd think and he fell for it too. He kinda grinned back and reached out for the bottle.

"Whiskey?" he said, sorta uncertain.

"Oh, no," I says sarcastic, "mother's milk. Good for you. Won't get pneumonia."

He began to color up agin, and then he took the pint and put it up, and jesus, he swallered about half of it. Just straight, runnin down his throat with him not swallerin. When he stopped he handed it back to me and grinned.

"Ain't you outa breath?" I asks. He dint even gasp which is moren I could do after that bigga drink.

"Hell, no," he says. "Us farm boys're raised on corn likker. Pop's got hisself a still and I sneak some every Sattiday night. Good stuff . . . Jack," he adds, friendly-like.

In about fifteen minutes we killed the bottle, and he's sittin there naked with that big john danglin down atween his legs—he was hung almost as big as I was. And I saw for all his braggin he wasn't as used to whiskey as he made out. He began to yawn a little, and purty soon he went over and picked hisself out a nice pile of hay and sorta laid back in it and closed his eyes.

The rain hadn't let up a'tall, and I was beginnin to get sleepy myself. The barn was hot as hell and the cool air dint come very far in the door. So I yawned a coupla times and he never stirred.

"I think I'll hit the hay too," I said, and sorta chuckled on account it really was hay this time, and he kinda mumbled and moved an arm back. He was layin there wide open, his cock sorta

39

swollen but not standin up, so I flops down on another pila hay just the other sidea him, and lays back and shuts my eyes.

Goddamn, it wasn't moren a minute till I heard his feet comin across the floor from his pila hay, and then he musta kinda sat down near me on account I could hear him breathin hard and short. I just kept my eyes closed and my hands behind my head, pertendin to be asleep, but I sorta arched my ass forward, sexy-like, and knowin the kid was right there beside me made me begin to git hard. I felt it risin slow and easy-like until it was standin straight up and I knew the kid was watchin it because he was hold-in his breath, until all of a sudden he couldn't hold it anymore, and he let it out in a kinda gasp, and then began to breathe hard and fast again. I could hear him even above the rain on the barn roof. Well, by then I was real stiff, stiff and standin straight up, and I made it throb just once so that the head swelled real big and red, as I knew it would. He saw it because he kinda gasped again.

Kids are funny, especially farm kids. Course they know all about sex, but they ain't had much experience with people. I could guess he admired my cock because it was big and clean and hard, and it kinda fascinates anybody who sees it, let alone gets a taste of it, on account I know how to use it okay. I may not got so many brains but I sure have learned how to fuck. Lotsa practice.

Anyway, after about a minnit, I felt his hand on my cock, just a kinda light little touch like a feather, and then he musta jerked his hand away agin. I made 'er jump agin, and sorta stirred, you know the way you do if somebody lays a hand on your cock while you're sleepin. All that's malarkey about people goin down on you while you're asleep — ain't nothin wakes you any quicker than somebody's hand or mouth on your cock.

Well, purty soon he puts his hand back on it, laid his thumb up alongside it and got it around the bottom with his fingers, and he sorta squeezed it a coupla times, and I answered him by makin it jump in his hand. He swallered hard and kept on workin it, and it was hard as a rock. But I kept my eyes closed until he began to feel sure I wouldn't wake up. Then it began to feel good, real good, and I thought Christ, I don't wanna come with him just jackin me off, so I opened my eyes wide without movin and looked right at him.

He dint see me at first. His lips was kinda parted and his eyes shinin and he was watchin my cock while he jacked it off. His own

40

cock was hard too, and standin up straight, the head as red as could be, and I could see a little sweat on his shoulders and back from the excitement.

Then I says, quiet-like, "Kinda like it, do yuh, kid?" and he jumped like he was shot and looked at me with big scared blue eyes. But he didn't let go of my cock. He wet his lips a little and says, "You sure got a big un."

I stuck my hips forward even more and strained aginst his hand. "Yuh want it?" I said, kinda lazy-like and lookin at him with my eyes half shut and me half-grinnin, and he swallered again and nodded, and said, "But wotta I do with it? I'll jack you off, huh?"

That did it. I swings my arms around from back my head and raised up. "Any ole day," I says, tough as I could. "What the hell you mean, jack off? That's for babies. Gimme a blowjob."

"Blowjob?" he says, kinda puzzled. "Like this?"

Honesta god, if the son of a bitch dint blow on it! Yeah, kinda gentle! I swore. "Goddammit," I said, "aincha never hearda blowjob? Go down on it, put yer mouth on it and suck it! Blow's just . . . just an expression."

He let go of it. "I ain't never done nothin like that," he says, scared-like.

I jumped up offn the hay. "By God," I says, "you ain't gonna be able to say that after today!" and I grabbed him by the shoulders and twisted him around so's I had my left leg agin his chest and my cock was jumpin there about six inches under his nose, and then I grabbed ahold his left wrist and at the same time grabbed his head with my left hand and shoved on it so's he was clamped there and couldn't move. Then I began to push him down to the head of my cock. He sure did fight back against me with his neck muscles and try to break away, but I held him fast.

He tried to talk me out of it and his voice sounded scared. "Jack . . . please! Jack, please don't! Honest, I ain't never done nothin like this before. Please, I'll jack you off—lemme do that."

"Nothin doin," I said. I kept forcin his head towards my cock. His neck muscles stood out and he was squirming like hell, tryin to pull loose. I laughed at him. "Christ, Eddie boy," I said, "what's a little cock gonna hurt you. You'll like it soon's you getta taste of it and feel it jumpin down yer throat. Ain't nobody ever been hurt by swingin on a good clean cock." His lips were clamped tight

41

shut, but I'd got his mouth down to 'bout a inch away. He kept twistin his head, and once he got it turned sidewise and looked up at me kinda beggin-like. He whimpered a little.

"You'd call me a cocksuck—" he began to say, and just then when his mouth was open I gave a hard shove on the back of his head, and the whole head of my cock jumped right inta his mouth. I could feel his teeth close down, and I knocked the back of his neck with my elbow. "Goddammit," I said, "you bite me and by jesus I'll beat your brains out. C'mon now—*suck!*"

The size of it and me pushin it was cuttin off his wind every time I hit the back of his throat, I could tell. And his eyes was waterin, but I sorta shifted position and got my left boot around his back, and pushed him down on his knees and arched my old ass forward so's he could get the benefit of all eight inches. I got both hands onna back of his head, and christ, it felt good. I was sockin it away and he was takin it without much complainin when I felt a kinda change in him. He stopped pushing against me with his arms, and slid one hand in atween my legs and started to play with my ass and grabbed my left leg around with his other arm, and then he got one finger in my asshole and did I go wild! God, anybody sticks his tongue or finger in my ass, I 'bout go off my nut.

He was beginnin to like it, that's fer sure. Just as I was 'bout ready to come, feeling that thrill all up and down my legs and in my belly, I saw a box 'bout ten feet away, and I yanked my cock outn his mouth and pulled him to his feet.

"What for?" he says. "You mad? I'll—I'll finish you," and he makes like to get down on his knees again, but I takes him by the shoulder and shoves him over to the box. "Git down on that," I says.

He looks at it. "How?" he says, puzzled.

"Git your back on it," I says, "and lay there with your head back. I'm gonna give you some reverse English." He did like I said. Then I stood t'other sidea the box and straddled his head and he opened his mouth, and began to push my old whang into his mouth like that. Dat's my favorite position—it kinda opens up a guy's throat, and you seem to be gettin in a lot deeper and further. I grabbed his head and kinda took holda his jaw where I could dig my fingers in along the sides. Then I started to fuck his mouth, slow and easy at first, and payin no attention to the stranglin

42

sounds he made. They got me even hotter than I been. He got his arms kinda in atween my legs and around my back and kept pullin me inta him steada trying to push me off.

I was beginnin to pump faster on him and my cock was swellin larger and I was about ready to blow. So was he, I guess. I saw his cock was purple at the head, and kinda angry red and its veins popping, and then—guess what! All of a sudden HE came, without me layin a hand on his cock, shootin right straight up, all over his belly, gobs and gobs of come, and his body jumped and quivered, and a big blob of come hit me right on the shoulder. I leaned over and licked it off, and just then I began to feel myself coming, and jesus! what a wad I shot inta him! I couldn't stop comin—he gagged on it and his mouth filled up, and it ran out the sides and down his neck and back over his shoulders. I ain't shot sucha load in a long time. And my butt muscles wouldn't stop working or my legs tightenin up, and me bent over holdin tight on his chin. He began to try to get up. I figgered he was gonna spit it out—MY come! and so I rammed my cock deep as I could and grabbed him under the chin, and one hand around the throat chokin him a little, and I says, "C'mon, damn you, swaller it, swaller all of it," and then I heard him swaller and it all went down. So that kinda satisfied me, cause nobody's gonna spit out any good come of mine if I know about it, so I began to take my cock out, real slow. He kinda slumped down from the box onta the hay on the floor, and he laid back against the box, pantin and outa breath, and his face wet from the tears I'd made come when I was forcin it in. His yaller hair was all mussed up, and I kinda felt sorry for him account the poor kid really hadda kinda rough time, especially this being his first experience. Sometimes I forget how big my cock is when I get hot—well, you know how the sayin goes, a stiff prick ain't got no conscience. So I goes to my kit and takes out a piecea rag and goes back to him with his chest still heavin and his eyes closed, and I begins to wipe the come offa his belly. His old cock was still dribblin all right; it was sorta bendin in the middle but still pullin out blobs of come. I guess I really din't wipe him off good wit the rag, just spread it around to make him feel sticky and then have it tighten up when it got dry

"Worn out, kid?" I asks him, on my knees in fronta him. He kinda opens one eye and nods on account he still can't speak. The

43

way he was sittin, wit his legs up, sorta brought up the cheeks of his tight brown little ass so's I could get a gander at 'em, and so help me god, if I dint start to get hard agin. Mebbe I never even stopped.

"Aw, you ain't had nothin yet," I says. "Dat's just a little appetizer. I'm gonna give you the real thing, huh? The real meat course."

Both his eyes popped open like as if he'd been goosed, wide open, but he dint look near as scared as he had been the first time. He kinda smiled. That was enough for me. I reached over and grabbed his two legs and threw 'em up in the air, and then caught him along the thighs afore he came down. That sure showed his asshole. There it was shinin out at me like a little brown eye, small and clean, and sorta squeezin itself together, y'know what I mean? Like as if it was waitin for what was comin and was still kinda scared of it. So I puts my face down between those two soft cheeks—and me not shaved, it musta scratched hell outa him—and he was hard again in no time. I stuck out my tongue and tasted that little hole. First I ran it all around the edges and watched it kinda jump back in, and then I really buried my face there, breathin hard, and rammed my tongue in as far's I could stick it, and wiggled the tip of it. The kid liked it. He was moanin with pleasure and groanin and also pushin his ass hard agin my face. Then I took my tongue out and licked his asshole the way you usta lick a lollipop—long slow licks up and down against it. Christ, he liked it!

He grabbed ahold my boot and pulled hard and that upset my balance and I kinda fell backward and his legs came down. He laid there pantin, and relaxed. I got up and put my hands under his armpits and gave a big heave-ho and lifted him up on the box. He just laid there kinda easy, one arm hangin down on the side. Well, I pushed his right leg aside, and lifted t'other one up on the box, and then I kneeled down agin and licked his asshole some more, only this time I lefta lotta spit layin there and also took my fingers and laid some more spit along my cock. Then, aholdin his legs apart, I went in.

Nothin hard at first, y'understand—real easy-like, givin that ole muscle a chance to relax without no trouble. He groaned once but kept his head flat and his eyes shut.

Christ, man—you ever screwed a boy? You have? Jesus, it's

44

great—lots bettern a woman, ain't it? Boys always stay tight on your cock, no loosenin' up like a cunt when she comes. Man, that kid was tops! I ain't never found a tighter cleaner little asshole. My cock fit in there like as if it'd been tailormade for it. I pushed it in slow, like I said, same speed, but makin sure it was all in, all eight inches, afore I stopped. I musta hit that gland in there, cause all of a sudden his body twitched like he was gonna come agin. But he dint.

It was kinda like layin it in warm leather, that got wet and shrunk down till it squeezed you real hard. Then I began to fuck him, long easy strokes. I'd bring it clear out almost, just to the tip, and then shove that big head as far in as it'd go. And I'd watch it as I drew it out, and see that hole expandin and squeezin tight like as if it didn't want to let go of it.

Gradually the spit dried offn it and—jeez, what a sensation, goin in dry! I knew I was hurtin him, but hell—by now I dint care. His head was turnin from side to side and he was groanin.

I can't come standin up like that, so I finally took my cock out, and then picked him up and held him—he kinda held onta me too, and I sat down on the box, and then I pulled his back against my belly, so's he was sorta settin in my lap with his ass above my prick. I got one of his legs doubled up and my arm under it, and then I reaches around him to squeeze his tit, and with the other hand I grabs ahold of his cock. Then I kinda eased him down until the head of my cock was just kissin his asshole. Then—wham! I pushed him down real hard on my cock—jeez, he hollered! and threw up his arms and grabbed one wrist and threw his head back—but I kept right on pushin, dry as it was, until it was inta the hilt. Man, how he was squeezin me in there!

Then I started rockin him—y'know? Me settin on the edge a the box and usin my leg muscles to rock him up and down. And I was jerkin him off the same time. I gives about three passes on his prick with my hand and whammo! Damned if he dint come again! Musta shot about eight feet in the air. And the squeezins his asshole gave my cock when he came made me come too, and my come inside him made the head of my cock all hot, hot as hell as it kept spitting out the last of it.

Then he just kinda fell apart, and I got up—quite a job, husky as he was, and I sorta staggered with him—my cock still in him, y'understand—over to the hay, and eased us both down on it. He was plumb tired out. I pulled my cock out real slow—it made a kinda hollow suckin sound, and wiped it offn a fistfulla hay. Then I laid down aside him and put my arm around him, and musta snoozed a minnit.

Anyways, when I woke up, by god iffn he dint have his head down there atween my legs, suckin me off for good and all, and seemin to enjoy the taste of his own shit on my cock. His old dong was right up by my face, and I no more started to lick it till bang! Off he went agin, all over my face. And just then I let fly, too, all over him.

Right then I happened to look up at the hayloft and whaddyuh think? Be damned if there wasn't another guy up there, jerkin hisself off all alone! Been watchin us all the time. "Hey!" I hollers up to him—"C'mon down and join the party!" So he gets up and starts downa ladder . . .

Huh? What's dat? Ain't you feelin' well, Mac? Oh . . . you can't take any more of it? Thought you liked to hear dirty stories. Jesus, just when I was gettin goin good . . .

Oh, you mean—not hear it here, in the bar? Naw, I don't mind. I'll go along with you. What kinda partment you got? Far? I gotta be back down at the Y sometime—get an early start tomorrow. By seven a.m. fer sure . . .

Hell, Mac, do I sound like as if I cared if you're queer. I'm itchy agin, mister—itchy all the time. What dyuh like to do? Okay, then—everything. Mebbe even a little piss inna mouth, huh? Good fer the digestion.

Okay, Mac—let's go.

Jungle Cat

The young man who came in the door was not what I expected. Usually, when Mike sent one over from the gym, they were somewhat run-of-the-mill. This one was not. He was no taller than I, and I am average; but there the likeness came to an end.

"You'll like Angelo," Mike had said over the phone. "He's from Puerto Rico."

"How much?" I asked.

"Only twenty," Mike said. "He's got a pachuco mark on his inner right calf. Had it on since he was a kid. Wants it off. Think you can do it?"

"Hardly," I said. "That's a doctor's work. I can put another design over it."

"Nope," Mike said. "He doesn't want that. He's a weightlifter, and you lose points if you have tattoodles. But you can talk to him about it."

"Okay," I said, and Mike hung up.

And sure enough, within twenty minutes Angelo was there. He stood rather tentatively in the shop, near the door. I looked him over quickly—and rather excitedly, my eyes tumbling happily up and down the crests and troughs of his blue black hair, and noting the careless little lock so carefully arranged to hang down on his somewhat low forehead. His lashes hardly belonged to a man's face, they were so long and black; and beneath them intense dark eyes looked just as thoroughly at me as mine at him. There were good male planes in his cheeks, and the skin stretched over them firmly. And what skin! Clear and unblemished, and tawny with the residue of the Caribbean sun left underneath it, with a darker red on the cheekbones where the summer sun had rested with contented familiarity, recognizing one of its own.

But it was the eyebrows that caught and held me. They grew in a straight and heavy line clear across the bridge of his nose, dipping slightly downward at the middle. They were the sort of thing that arrests the eye without at once relaying to the mind the source of the great attractiveness. They were calm, but with a sense of mobility in them. Fascinated, I watched as one of the dark lines shot up like a startled bird from cover, and then he moved towards me with an outstretched hand.

"My name's Angelo," he said, and I shook his hand. The grasp was strong. "Mike sent me over."

I let out my breath so that he heard me. He looked a bit surprised. "Something wrong?"

"No," I said, "nothing at all. Mike's sent over several, but scarcely anything like this up to now."

He grinned—a startling effect, with his teeth so white against the dark of his skin. "Aw," he said sardonically, "I bet you say that to all the boys."

"No," said I, "first time today."

And the small inconsequential talk went on for a few minutes— a kind of investigative nuzzling of each other, much like two dogs meeting for the first time, to find out if they can be friends, lovers, or just ordinary airedales together. He had come from Puerto Rico when he was fourteen, gone to school and graduated, played the drums and sung with a small combo; he wanted to write music, had no steady girl friend, and had never heard of Sibelius. He pulled up his trousers on a strong young leg, covered with fine black hair, to show me the deep scarred cross of his pachuco mark with three rays tattooed into his skin.

I shook my head. "Probably have to have a skin graft over it since it's more than three years old," I said. "And that would mean another piece of skin off your butt. Mike said you didn't want another design to cover it. A black panther would, maybe." He reminded me of one.

"No," he said, "guess not." He pulled his trouser leg down. His slacks were dark, and he wore a light checked windbreaker over a bright red nylon T-shirt. The red was another skin; his handsome pectoral muscles swelled beneath the scarlet of the fabric. I noticed that his pants were pegged to a narrow band at the ankles, and his shoes looked vaguely Italian; where in the world did these Puerto Rican boys get their odd clothes? But strangely—whether it was the overwhelming force of his dark handsomeness, or his personality, or my momentary breathlessness at the sight of him—Angelo, I thought, looked good in them.

Getting over the hurdle of the first few moments with these young men who sell themselves is always a little embarrassing for me. The moment of silence prolonged itself, until I said somewhat nervously, "Well, shall we . . . er . . . retire to the back room?" Banal and trite!

"Sure," he said, "whenever you want."

My mouth was dry as I went to the front door, and stuck in the edge of it a small sign saying: "Out to Eat; Back in 20 Minutes." For a moment, I glimpsed the fragile span of the Bay Bridge glittering in the afternoon sun, and unaccountably winked at it. Then I locked the door and followed him into the back room, drawing the curtains together. In the shabby old storeroom with the bed, bench, and desk, the high ceiling and the boxes piled everywhere—well, it was an unhappy contrast to love under the blue and golden skies of Greece, or on the white sands of Italy. I arranged the desk lamp to hide my defects and to illuminate him. And then my hesitations drowned themselves in his youth and firmness, and we might as well have been together—and alone—on the isles beneath the wind, with the warm dark night around us, and the ice-cold moon above.

Who can say at what moment love begins, or when it ends? Indeed, who can say of what it is compounded? It is said that it sometimes comes swiftly upon one, like a plague, consuming and devouring, and turning the mind and body black with its fires; and it is also said that at other times its approach is soft and gentle, unperceived, slow and unfelt. I was under no illusions with Angelo. He would call, come, and collect—and the fact that he often hung around the shop afterwards did not make me think he found a father-image in me, nor that his lively black eyes even really saw me—or if they did, it was through a shimmering veil composed of

49

dollar signs and tidy entries in a bankbook.

But hang around he did. He would sit singing for hours—thumping an old wooden box in lieu of his bongo drums, singing in a husky though fairly able baritone all of the collection of modern songs, especially rock 'n' roll ones of which he was very fond. Or he would sit combing his glossy hair in front of the mirror, chair tilted back and comb busy, until his fingers helped his hair to find its proper and pleasing wave—and then with a small flick, he would twist his forelock until it fell just right down towards those incredible eyebrows.

"You ever shave between your eyebrows and you needn't come around here any more," I said.

In those first excited and exciting contacts of ours, I came to know his body as well as a sulptor knows his marble. It was really magnificent, and he was proud as a peacock of it. He liked to pose naked in front of the full-length mirror. His shoulders were practically one-and-a-half to the ratio of his hips' one-half; there were four strong ridges in his abdomen, and he loved to draw his arm down to the side, tensing it so that his triceps leaped into a golden mountain. At the base of his spine, some fine small body hair drew inwards toward the column in an even pattern, as if a strong wind had blown it so, or water washed over it.

Little by little he learned to forsake the passivity he had at first, when—with eyes closed and forearm flung across them—he dreamed of something else instead of what was going on. To tell the truth, he didn't like the idea of any of it at all. But he took to my suggestions quickly (after all, who was paying?) and even enthusiastically, so that often—crisscrossed and sweating—I had to beg him to stop. He hated people like me—you could tell that by the enthusiasm of his violence—but he had to live. And this was an easier way to make money than to work. You made more quicker.

He was moody and mercurial, as most Latins are; and when he was angry, you could almost see the inch-long lightnings flash from his eyes. One day he came into the shop, very cross. It was hard to find out what was wrong. Finally it began to come out.

"Had a fight with my uncle," he said. "Carlo." He didn't look at me, but at the floor.

"Why?" I asked. "What about?"

"Nuthin'," he said.

I did not like Carlo at all. Although he was Angelo's uncle, he was not many years older. He sometimes came with Angelo into the shop, and his whole attitude was too protective, like that of a mother-hen or a Methodist aunt. I disliked his quick and darting eyes, his mean little ways, and the fact that he spoke such broken English that I could barely understand him; whereas Angelo spoke perfect West Coast.

There were one or two violent scenes in my shop, when Carlo followed Angelo down to see me. The rapid Spanish was too much for me, but I caught the words 'mamador' and 'maricon' and 'no me jolas' flung around in fury. Carlo once threw himself on the bed in the backroom and wept, and once Angelo hit him in the kidney, so that there was blood for days thereafter. And through it all I watched with as much calm detachment as I could, feeling very slimy myself, for I had begun to suspect that my motives were not so pure as I had thought them at first. Perhaps it was my dirty resolve that if I could not have him for my own (and no man could), then Carlo wasn't going to have him either.

And finally Angelo's father began to suspect the truth. In a characteristic Latin reaction he suggested only that Carlo move out of the house and get his own apartment, and that was all there was to it—no threats of prosecution, no violence—just a Puerto Rican acknowledgment of a fact, and a small gesture made about it.

We felt that we had won.

Things should have calmed down a little after that, but life with Angelo was always stormy. His rages were unpredictable, and my own temper was often short. Although he was scrupulously honest, in that he never stole anything, as we grew to know each other better, he began to take for granted that what was mine was his. He was one of the 'gimme' boys—"Gimme this, gimme that"—and usually I gave it to him, if not at first then later.

But living on the brink of a volcano is always a little exciting, and my shop was at the edge of Vesuvius. Sometimes there was a sudden explosion.

The matter of the combs, for instance.

Angelo couldn't keep a comb, or a cigarette lighter, for more than a week. Heaven knows what he did with them, but they were always disappearing. In my shop I always kept an extra one, for those days when I left mine on the dresser-top at home. I liked a little all-steel Swedish comb. Angelo's eyes lit up when he saw the first one.

"Gimme it, will you?"

"Oh, all right," I said, "you'll just lose it."

"No, I won't," he said.

"You're just like a magpie," I said. "If you see something shiny, you've got to have it."

Three days later, he opened the drawer and put my second newly purchased reserve comb in his pocket again, grinning at me.

"So you did lose it," I said. "They cost two dollars."

He laughed. And then a few days later, it happened again. "Listen," I said, "I don't mind the money so much, but I hate like hell to be running over to buy another one every time I turn around."

"Buy 'em by the dozen," he laughed. "Besides, the exercise is good for you."

It went on happening. On the seventh or eighth time, when he reached for the comb in the drawer, I got up and went to him and without a word took it from his hand and put it into my pocket. He was so surprised at the gesture that he did not hold on to it. Then he recovered.

"C'mon," he said, "gimme it. I promise I'll never lose another one."

"Nonsense," I said.

From out of the west the storm arrived. There was no herald, no thunder, no dark cloud. One moment he was smiling, and the next—his brows drew down and together and his lips tightened into a snarl, and the little lightnings flashed from his eyes.

"You mean you're not gonna give me that goddamned lousy comb?"

"No," I said, more calmly than I felt.

He took a handful of change out of his pocket and flung it straight down on the floor. It scattered in every direction, and one nickel rolled under the stove. "There!" he said. "There's some money for your goddamned combs!" In a rage, he strode to the clothes closet, opened the door, and yanked down a sportscoat and shirt that he had left hanging there, and threw them over his arm. "I'm gettin' out!" he snarled. "You can keep your lousy

52

combs from now on!"

"Angelo—" I began, baffled. There was nothing I could think of to stop the progress of the tornado.

"*Goodbye!*" he shouted, and went out the door. He tried to slam it, but the heavy doorcheck spoiled his dramatic exit. I stood there trembling. He'll be back, I thought to myself; he needs the money. And then I remembered his pride, and his dozens of other clients. Oh, well—you'll save some money, I thought. But you'll miss him.

I need not have worried too much. He came in the next day and sat down. "I can't apologize," he said. "I ain't made that way. But here I am."

I looked at him. "You'll bust a blood vessel some day if you keep that up." And then it was all over.

I never tired of looking at Angelo's body. It was classic, the kind of form that would have delighted any sculptor—Praxiteles, perhaps, who could have created another faun from him. Sometimes Angelo annoyed me with his childish enthusiasms, but I never had enough of watching him. His hands were exceptionally beautiful, his long slim brown fingers, closing over the handle of a Mexican child's toy, repeated in miniature the beauty of his body, exquisitely perfect. Or as he kneeled above me . . . and I looked upwards at the incredible landscape of his abdomen and chest, watching the deep brows drawn together in concentration, or—seen from this angle—the almost baby-Latin face, the perfectly modeled lips with the under one drawn in a little, and the almost hypnotic pattern of the rapidly moving muscles of his right arm and shoulder— well, these were things I was busily photographing upon the inexhaustible plates of my mental camera, to develop later and cherish through all my life.

And then suddenly it all came to a dull and thudding end.

Angelo came in one day. We talked for a little while, but he seemed distracted.

"What's the matter, kiddo?" I asked him at last.

He bit his underlip. "I must've strained myself up at the gym," he said, and he described the symptoms.

I shook my head. "Oh-oh," I said. "It's the doctor for you, me bucko."

"You think it is . . .?"

53

"He'll tell you," I said. "But don't delay. Where'd you get it?"

He shook his head, miserable. "I dunno," he said. And then he got up and struck his fist into his hand. "Damn it, and just when things were goin' so good."

"One of the hazards of the profession," I said, as calmly as I could. And then I gave him some money for the injection and sent him away.

I remember once reading in the pages of a French novel something to the effect that luckily there were those who preferred the 'mal-foutus,' the poorly-put-together ones—and who gave them some pleasure in life. And I must confess that I found a certain perverse attractiveness in the 'broken vessels'—persons missing a finger, or an arm . . . But Angelo's particular method of breaking the vessel was the one thing which I could not stand. It would take me months before I could bring myself to touch him again, no matter how quickly he was cured.

After that, I saw him only once. He came in to announce that he was leaving for Redondo Beach, to live with some wealthy guy who had asked him. There had been trouble at home—his father making financial demands, his mother scolding, and Carlo after him with increased vigor.

"I can't stand it any longer," he said. "I'm old enough now to be on my own."

I could not resist a faint bitterness as I said. "You call this being on your own?"

"Well," he said, "perhaps I should just have said 'away from home.' " Then he paused, and made a little backward movement with his head, to indicate the back room. "Do you wanna—?"

Carefully I explained to him why I still could not yet. He flushed, and looked at his elegantly pointed shoes. "Well . . ." he said.

"But let me watch you just once more," I said, and he nodded.

And then he lay on the bed in the back room, and I sat in the chair behind him. I looked for a last time at the long tawny flanks of my jungle cat, my black panther; watched the pattern of his muscles as his arm moved, and saw again the arched foot, with tensed toes pointing downward, the tight-clenched eyes—and then after a little while I could no longer see what was happening because my vision was so blurred.

54

Who can say at what moment love begins, or when it ends?

Now, when I leave the shop and go home, I look at my statues, I listen to my music, and then I go to bed. I sleep on my left side and put my left hand, palm up, under the pillow beneath my head. And then for some reason—perhaps a childish one long buried—I reach up with my right hand and clasp it around my left wrist. And at that moment, I always think of Angelo.

Bits of news reach me from time to time—oddly enough, brought to me by Carlo. Angelo is about to have a record pressed by one of the big companies, he drives a fine new car (but not his own), he has new clothes but no pocket money. . .

And in the last half-conscious moment before I go to sleep, I sometimes wonder if Angelo could get away from his Redondo bitch long enough to go to Tokyo with me next Christmas . . .

Baby Tiger

I

"C'mon," said Mike, standing in the middle of the shop, legs apart. "Close this joint up, and let's get the hell outa here. You need some fresh air."

I sighed, looked over at Dave and winked. "You're completely upsetting my life," I complained. "Until you came along, things were peaceful. I got up every morning, opened my shop at noon, and went straight home to bed every midnight. I—"

"Yeah, I know," Mike said. "You were sure gettin' in a rut. When you used to be a newspaper reporter, you prob'ly went out more." He shook his head in mock sadness.

"At least I never wasted my time going to the movies," I said. "And drive-ins! You have ruined me completely."

Dave laughed. "I'm afraid decay had already set in," he said. "And as for ruin—what could anyone do to ruin an old broken-down tattoo artist anyway?"

Insult on insult! But they were quite right, except I didn't think I was broken down. It had been a shock to all my friends, both in and out of the newspaper world, when I gave up working on the paper in disgust, tired of the harness, and certain that the experiment of the public press in America was a failure, its motives questionable, its readers too easily led by the nose. By all rights I should have gone into something decent, like editing or writing for encyclopedias. Instead, with a kind of suicidal rejection and scorn for middle-class opinion, I took up the most suspect of all

56

'professions' in America, the one that balances itself delicately on the thin edge between the legal and the illegal, and became a tattoo artist. And all too soon I discovered that I had but exchanged one sort of martyrdom for another, and even a worse one. When I was on the paper, I could look at the copy boys and admire them, but never touch. And now—well, I could touch: arms and chests, perhaps, with my fingers feeling the sweat in the little bramble patch of the armpit, or brushing across the perfect smooth plateau of a young chest—but all this in the line of duty. My secret had to be kept even more carefully than ever before—if I wanted to continue to make any money.

A young hoodlum with a ducktail haircut, dressed in a leather jacket and levis, strolled past the glass walls of my shop, looking at the designs; and two sailors peeked into the arcade from Market Street.

Mike said, "More business?" and I said, "Just lookers, I think." A few years of experience in the game had enabled me to tell who wanted a tattoo and who didn't, and had even helped me to judge with reasonable accuracy how much money a person had in his pocket. As for the little Ivy League boys in suits, and the college kids—no, they never bought. Slummers all, they came to see how the other half lived, and might well have been surprised to find out how well.

Dave was a little restless. He always was. Some inner motor kept him ever on the go. He had a dark and handsome face, a kind of Italian mixture, and was rather stocky. He was an artist whose work Mike marketed, and a pianist, and even a writer now and then. You would scarcely have thought it possible that the two of them had lived together for eight years. Of course, they weren't faithful to each other; they did what they wanted, but always there was the tie—or the habit—that kept them sailing happily along, with due regard to the policeman around the corner.

You could divide all guys into two classes, sweetie pies and baby tigers. Dave belonged to the first. He wrote the letters and knew how to spell the words.

Mike was the baby tiger. Baby tigers never read anything but the headlines and the comic pages; they can't spell, but they can do arithmetic and fix sparkplugs. And they never, never write letters to anyone. These two in their living together complemented each other like red and green. If one of them couldn't do something, the other could.

The three 'customers' had disappeared as I knew they would. "C'mon, get the needles put away," said Mike, and I closed up the shop and left with them.

The night was wonderful, as it always was in May. The lights of the bridges glittered in their arcing path across the bay; the air was clean and fresh and a little salty, and was blowing cool. Mike zipped up his motorcycle jacket, hoisted his chino pants with a sailor's gesture—flat of the hand forward and back—and kicked me playfully on the shin with his heavy black boot.

"Thanks," I said. And then laughing, he reached out and through my shirt took hold of my left nipple and twisted hard.

"If you two are going to make love," said Dave, "I'll go to the Ramrod and see what's cooking."

I rubbed my smarting flesh. "No chance," said I. "Not with this big gook. Besides, he's not nearly tough enough to suit me. Reminds me of a big genial lovable Boy Scout troop leader. Hasn't got the brains of a jackass."

Mike had another trick he was always pulling; he'd grab your hand with one of his big paws, and hold your fingers straight, then with the other hand he'd bend your thumb down in. He did it now. "Take it back," he said.

"Ow," I said. "All right—I take it back. You have got the brains of a jackass."

The pressure increased; I was bent nearly double. A woman on the street looked at us curiously. "Take it all back," said Mike. "Say 'uncle.' "

"Uncle!" I gasped and he let go.

Well, it was like that—harmless fun and games. There was not even any special undertone to it all. We had been friends for a year and a half; I had never 'bothered' either of them, and they—needless to say—hadn't me. We'd gone every Sunday night to a drive-in theater; we'd eaten approximately one meal a day together.

I had found the baby tiger appealing in a kind of sexless way. I like all types of people, except the very rich, who are mostly phonies; and the stewbums, who are lazy.

But something had happened to Mike a few months ago that turned him into a fascinating creature in my eyes. It had been partly my fault. Mike had always shown a certain extrovert aggressiveness; he was the one who could approach and talk to people. Dave and I were always tongue-tied, and shied away from contact with strangers. So Mike did all the conversation, and we reaped the pleasure. But that one evening I had a friend visiting me from the east, and introduced him to Mike. This meeting was like a sudden opening of a door in Mike, an unexpected outflowing of a strange dark wave of enjoyment in mastering another personality, in compelling him to do his absolute bidding. The door led to S/M.

From that point on, he was a changed person. I had heard such a thing could happen suddenly—but overnight! I watched the growth of his new pattern with the same hypnotized immobility a person is supposed to have when faced with a cobra.

And the conversations! I had had some little experience along the line of his new interest, being old and full of sin; and almost daily he asked me questions: Why is this? What makes them afraid? Why do they get so angry? Why do they do what I tell them? Why do they always want to come back for more? Why do they taunt me when they know they'll pay for it?

I answered him as best I could, but I soon ran out of information. And then he began to bring me reports, new experiments, new persons he had met, new desires. How his eyes glowed when he talked—and how dry my mouth sometimes became!

"Mike," I said to him at one point, "I don't know much about these things, really I don't. I've been on this side of the fence just psychically in the past; I really can't explain. And it was never an absorbing interest with me, never a thing that I actively engaged in. Or at least, not to a very great extent," I added, remembering.

He laughed. I looked at him, marveling at the change that a few weeks had made in him—a real physical change. He had eyes that could hood themselves like a falcon's, narrowing down to a danger-line; he had always been good-looking—tall, blond, and lean. Now he seemed to be filling out. He looked as aggressively masculine and cruel as a hunting panther—or better, a full-grown tiger now. His lips seemed to have darkened in color, and his eyes grown deeper blue; out of him came an aura that you could almost touch, something dark and sinister and ancient as hell.

"Don't kid me," he said, and he reached over and pinched me, hard. I winced, but didn't cry out. He laughed again. "I kinda think you might like to hear a concerto in the music room yourself."

Doubletalk—I didn't know exactly where it came from, but I knew what he meant. His 'music room' was the cellar of the house where he and Dave lived. He had fixed it up as a gym, long before his new self emerged. And so it was full of slanting exercise boards, benches bolted to the floor, rings set in the wall, overhead weights and pulleys, and all the rest.

I shuddered faintly. "Not me," I said. "I'll just be content to read the reviews. Besides," I said, teasing him with a private joke, "I don't care for beginners. No amateur musicales for me."

The word 'beginner' always got him. If it did not exactly irritate him, at least it made him fidget, almost with embarrassment. He gritted his teeth. "Beginner, huh! You'd be surprised. If I just got you once in the music room, alone, I'd show you I could do more than carry a tune. And listen, let me tell you something—" He leaned forward and gripped my knee. "One of these days I will. I know your type. You're just cryin' for it."

"The hell I am," I said. I had my pride. "And don't worry, you haven't got a fat chance of ever luring me into your den."

"Wanna bet?" he said.

"Yeah," I said. "A dollar."

He grinned. "Okay, cheapskate," he said. "You're on!"

We left it at that.

Who is to say what song the sirens sang, or what name Achilles assumed when he hid among the women? Or at what point there began to grow, deep inside me, the wild spore? And when did that spore burst, and scatter its mobile seeds into my blood?

Whatever and whenever it happened to me, the progress was slow and gradual. It came by littles; they were sly-footed, those little seeds, as they flowed along my veins. When I looked for them, they were not there—or perhaps they wore the common-place mask of camaraderie and friendship. But they spread throughout my system, secretly and insidiously as a virus. The disease fed on the tales that Mike continued to tell me, for there is nothing that glazes over the soul and keeps it enthralled more than those tales. It was nourished by the dreadful nearness of his body, and the smell of his leather jacket. He was always pummeling me, cracking my fingers, hitting me on the shoulder, rubbing my ear flat against my head — all in the name of good healthy American-style buddy-boy horseplay. Or was it?

And suddenly I wakened one morning to find myself trapped completely. In one of those moments of clarity, when we are privileged — or forced — to look deep into the well of self, I saw what lay at the bottom, and knew what I wanted.

But I am proud. I could not make a direct revelation. And so I began my tricks, and, though I hated myself for it, I found myself following the classic pattern that you can find in any elementary text on psychiatry. A strange kind of twisted, negative aggressiveness began to appear in me. I knew that Mike did not really care for me except as a friend; if my name were added to the growing list of people in his stable, it would be another puff for his ego — and that realization made me more than ever resolved to silence. And so I listened to his stories, which grew more and more painful to me the more jealous I became of the inmates of his stable, like little Gerhardt for instance. Mike liked Gerhardt, who was an East German refugee, and cooked in a bank's cafeteria. Mike had picked him up in a bar one night, noting with his new perceptiveness how the blond kid had followed him with his eyes, taking in all the details of boots and jacket and key-'chain' of leather thong tied in a hangman's knot. Gerhardt fell for Mike, much against his will; for Gary was on the verge of going to New York, where a wealthy score had offered him ease and riches for a very long time. But the kid, though fighting as hard as he could, was not able to break away.

"For the love of Mike—" I began. That wasn't right; I started over. "For the love of Pete, Mike," I said when he told me this story with glinting eyes. "Why don't you let him go?"

Mike looked genuinely astonished. "Are you kiddin'? Let him go? Never, not on your life. I want him right where he is, in my stable."

And then the abyss closed, but I had seen down into it.

It was a chilling story, and it made me unhappy. Yet had he suddenly cut off his narratives, the distress would have been intolerable.

There is no doubt that I inflicted myself upon him with increasing frequency. I saw this forcing as a kind of magic gesture, devised to call his attention to me more, to get him to change his mind and give me a proof of interest. I behaved as if I were presenting him with an old unpaid bill for affection. I knew he disliked it. Wasn't I his good ole buddy? Didn't I have his attention?

But Mike was by no means stupid. Intuitively he knew what was going on. I had to set the stage very subtly in my attempts to provoke him into a sign.

There was that time I had to go to Sacramento to get some tattoo colors from a friend, and some other supplies. A week before I left, one evening, I mentioned it to Mike.

"You mean you're actually gonna shut the joint and mebbe lose a three-buck job?"

"Yeah," I said, "it'll break my heart, but I gotta go."

And then I didn't mention it again. On the evening before I was to go, I went with him and Dave to a movie, and resolutely kept quiet. The next morning I left early, and didn't get back until five in the afternoon, instead of twelve when I usually opened the shop. At ten minutes after five, Mike burst into the arcade. Lightning played around his head; two-foot flames were bursting from his ears.

"Just where the hell have you been?" he grated at me.

The spectacle was terrifying. Suddenly he seemed about seven feet tall—diabolic, his mouth hard and cruel, his eyes smoldering. I gulped. He slammed his fist into my shoulder.

"I—told you," I said. "I had to go see old Kurtsworth, to get some colors. I—I told you last week, and then—" I said, warming to my story, "I told you again last night, just before we went into the movie. You weren't listening," I said accusingly. Counterattack is the best defense.

"You didn't tell me last night!" he said. "You didn't say a word about it."

It was a tense moment. "I did too," I lied. "You just didn't hear me. You remember I talked to you last week about it too." He had grabbed my shoulder, and now I felt his grip relaxing. He let go. "Yeah," he said, "I remember that. But I sure don't remember you saying anything last night."

Well, I won that round. There was my little proof. But the more I thought about it, the more ashamed I was. What was happening to me? What had made me play such a shabby little trick? Well, the answer was simple. I needed attention, and I felt the strong drive

62

inside me to punish him because he didn't think me worthy. I marketed my suffering by an exhibition of martyrdom, but at what a price to my ego . . .

The weeks went by. I kept busy, industriously building my little sand traps and deadfalls for Mike. Some of them he fell for, but I am afraid that gradually he began to see through most of them.

And then the headaches began. Any fool would know why. The human organism can stand only so much tension. And the embarrassing thing was that they hit me only briefly, at the peak of pleasure. There was a long to-do over that, with a doctor Mike knew furnishing me with some tranquilizers that cured the headaches, but did not ease the essential ache that caused them. Mike watched me with a cool calculating detachment, with what dark plots scuttering through the grey shadowy valleys of his brain, I'll never know.

Dave helped to clear the air somewhat. He came to see me one day, and gradually eased around into the subject. "I know it's really none of my business," he said, "but why don't you just give way once and get it out of your system? Mike wants you to come over to dinner tomorrow night," he said, "after you close the shop."

That pleased me—'Mike wants.' I took it as another proof of interest. And so the next night, quite happily, I went to their house.

Mike was alone in the living room. The curtains were drawn. "Where's Dave?" I said as I took off my jacket. Mike grinned. He was in full uniform—black jacket, boots, chino trousers, and very handsome. "He got a sudden call for rehearsal," Mike said, "and he won't be back until after midnight."

There was a slight feeling of uneasiness in me. "You mean to say," I said, half jokingly, "that I am alone in this house with you?"

"Yup," said Mike. He paused. "And this is it, kid!" He bit it out.

Terror exploded in me like a rocket, so violent and intense that my vision flickered for a moment. I jumped to my feet and took three involuntary rushing steps to the door. But Mike was ahead of me. He stood with his back against it, and his arms folded. I backed away, thinking that it must all look like a very bad movie. The scene was frozen in my mind, photographed and stored away forever.

63

"M—Mike," I said, my throat so dry I could only rasp. "Mike—no. I mean—not so suddenly. I—I'm not prepared for this. I—I need more time to think. I—"

Mike laughed. He came and put his arm around my neck and rubbed the leather sleeve under my nose affectionately. "Why, boy—what's to be afraid of? Nothin's gonna hurt you at all. Don't think—that's what the trouble is. We'll just have a nice little chat, mebbe listen to a little music. You know we're much too good friends. I couldn't hurt you."

I was almost blubbering with fear. The gentleness was phony, I knew—the kind of deceptive mildness he had used on others, shortly before he whopped the daylights out of them. "Just calm down now, boy," he said. "We can't let you go on makin' yourself sick, now, can we?" He moved me towards the sofa, and sat me down; then turned off all but one light. "Now, you just be a good boy. Relax. Take some of your things off. It's too hot in here."

What did they feel, those poor unfortunate ones at the guillotine, as they were strapped to the board, and slowly lowered into a horizontal position? My tongue stuck to the roof of my mouth, there was a faraway buzzing in my ears, and the great vein in my throat chugged heavily. I felt as lost and alone as the man who sees the shores of home fade for the last time, and knows he will not return.

My wallet fell out of my trousers; the sound of it hitting the floor in the quiet room was like a small muffled explosion. Mike picked it up, opened it, and extracted a one-dollar bill. He stuck it slowly into his pocket, and grinned. His face was that of Mephisto in the half-light.

"The buck you owe me," he said. "Remember?" And then he opened the other door in the room, and stood aside, and made an ironic usher's gesture towards the black opening.

Trembling, lost, and with my skin chilling in the wave of dank cold air, I started down the steps.

II

"Do you think I fit into my new stall all right?" I asked, looking around my shop. It was the same shabby little tattoo shop, with the design boards that had begun to turn brown.

Mike was straddling the customer's chair, resting his folded arms on the back. "Yeah," he said, "you look real natural in it." He glanced around. "Only see that you keep it swept out," he said, "and *clean!* You can't tell when the boss'll want to take the old nag out for a canter."

He unfolded himself from the chair and stood up, almost brushing the ceiling, or so it seemed. "Well, I gotta run along. Gotta heavy date," he said. "New one off a pineapple boat."

"You find them everywhere," I said, feeling a sour juice of jealousy spill over inside.

"So long," he said and flicked a finger at the brim of his visored cap.

It was scarcely a matter that many people gave much thought to these days, but during the past few weeks I had been considering the slave mentality. History is full of the bloody oppressions visited upon slaves in all periods — but it has very little to say about the ones that were contented. Undoubtedly there were many in ancient Athens that did not chafe at their bondage. And I fancy that even the most spirited racehorse can easily develop an affection for the harness, if he has a good master.

The trouble was, I wasn't exactly sure mine was a good one. The first two weeks after the concerto had been happy enough. It didn't matter to me whether I saw Mike during those days. I felt like old Wordsworth visiting Tintern Abbey, realizing that he would in the future draw enough nourishment from his experience to keep him happy for many years. But then when Mike began to come around again, I thought I sensed a difference in him. It was not that he took me too much for granted; it was that he didn't take me at all. He hardly noticed me. I felt very sensitive about it, thinking that perhaps I had been too much afraid that night. But as the weeks became a month, I grew more aware of Mike's coldness. It was obvious and definitive: now that I was safely installed, he had forgotten me.

When Mike came back to the shop a couple of hours later, I was still puttering around. He had someone with him — the boy from the pineapple boat, a really spectacular person, almost as tall as Mike, and much more muscular. He wore a Navy watch cap pushed back upon blue-black curls, and his face was swarthy, the chin deeply cleft. He had on a pair of wide-flaring sailor's dungarees, and dirty blue sneakers on his feet. The horizontal blue stripes of a

French sailor's *loup-de-mer* circled dizzyingly around a broad and bursting chest, and the long sleeves of the shirt were pushed up to the elbows, showing his brawny and tanned forearms. He looked almost gypsy; an earring would not have been out of place. His teeth flashed brilliantly in the dark copper of his face. And when he came into the shop, the air almost crackled with his personal magnetism. Beside him, Mike looked a bit pallid; anyone would have.

"Glad you're still here," said Mike. "This is Rafe. He's Portuguese, and don't speak the English much, hey, Rafe?"

I had my hand extended to shake Rafe's, and the boy was just beginning the motion forward with his hand, a big grin on his face, when Mike hit him once sharply in the middle of the forearm, knocking his hand downwards.

We never connected. There seemed to be a sudden cutoff of the sailor's magnetism. He made a small sidewise gesture of his head — not much of a gesture at all, but a kind of inner wilting. And the eyes he turned up to Mike no longer flashed their black male fire, but had melted into a kind of womanly softness. I thought for an instant that he was going to lay his head on Mike's shoulder. Then the moment passed. Mike shook his shoulder a little, lowered his eyelids and said: "Just wanted you to meet the kid. He wants a tattoo. I'll bring him in tomorrow for it. A quirt." He turned to Rafe. "Go out and look at the designs a minute, kid," he said, and Rafe went.

Mike turned back to me. "I want you to make the handle short, and then twist the braiding around so it makes my initials." He laughed. "Then he'll know he belongs to me every time he looks at it."

"Okay," I said noncommittally. Like priests and psychiatrists, tattoo artists cannot be shocked. Then I said, "Seems like something's wrong here, Mike. You sure this boy's on my side of the fence?"

"Absolutely." Mike gave a sharp harsh laugh. "Maybe hard to believe, but he's there completely."

"The way he looks," I said, "so male, so dominating . . ."

Mike laughed again. "Appearances are deceivin', ain't they, buddy?" And he gave me a high hard pinch. "Still," he said thoughtfully, "sometimes I kinda wonder what it's like, on your side. Right guy comes along some time, I wanna try it and see."

That left me speechless. I couldn't believe that Mike could ever be interested in such an experience. Life was getting too complicated and contradictory. Then Mike flicked a goodbye, and Rafe — all male again — flashed another Hollywood smile at me, and they went out into the night.

I spent an hour the next morning designing the thing Mike wanted — and in the middle of my work, a happy little idea occurred to me. So I changed the design a trifle — Mike's initials were still there — but now, every time a mirror would show Rafe his tattoo, the mirror image would let him see my own initials as well.

They came in during the early afternoon. "He's scared," Mike said. He punched Rafe affectionately. "Where you want the tattoo, ole boy?"

Rafe put one huge paw on his left shoulder. "Here," he said. "High up." And he grinned at me like a school kid.

"All right," I said, "take your shirt off." He had on the same French *loup-de-mer*. A sudden look of fright came into the boy's eyes. "No, no!" he said violently. "Put — here," and he slid the sleeve up over his forearm.

"Hell!" said Mike, striding forward. "You want it on the shoulder — *get it there!* You think this guy's never seen anything like your back before?"

He yanked Rafe roughly to his feet, although I am sure Rafe could have flattened him with one good punch, and grabbing hold of the striped shirt, in one quick movement pulled it over the Portuguese boy's head.

I stared silently at his back, crisscrossed with bright red welts.

Mike grunted. "Looks like you fell over a barbed wire fence last night, kid." Then he turned to me. "Okay, get goin'."

When my fingers closed around the boy's magnificent deltoid, I could feel what my eye could take in: his whole body was trembling faintly, gently, and the skin was covered with a thin film of sweat. He had his head lowered almost on his chest, and his eyes were closed. And so he sat through the whole operation, which lasted about ten minutes. The little tremor went on during all that time, as if a small vibrating motor were running somewhere inside him.

When it was finished, Mike seized the boy's shoulder and looked at it. "Damned good job," he said. The boy nodded, too, and smiled a little shyly at me. "I like," he said, but he turned his head as he spoke, so that he was looking at Mike, and not at my work of 'art.' And then they were gone, out into the hot sun that crinkled up from the pavements.

It was midsummer, but from that day there began the winter of my discontent. I was not much older than Mike, but I was old enough to feel that I had earned my victories, the hard way, from experience. Up to how I had looked on myself as a free soul, detached from all wounding entanglements and encounters. And I had believed, wrongly, that the one time with Mike would be enough.

Now I felt bonds grow tighter. With a dead heart, such as I thought I had, there could never be any possibility for me of 'falling in love'; I had the usual butterfly nature of the majority of our group. It was a *carpe diem* philosophy I followed, or perhaps *carpe hominem* . . . But there was a terrible urgency inside me to get Mike to say yes once more. It grew as the summer grew.

"Never again?" I asked him when he was in the shop one evening.

He made an impatient gesture. "Oh, yeah," he said, "but I ain't been in the mood lately." He had a troublesome sinus, and the doctor had injected some kind of medication into it recently. "After I get over this trouble wit' my schnoz," he said.

But he got over it, and then there was always something else — a half dozen promises, and as many postponements, or else forgetting. "Are we too good friends?" I asked again.

"Sure — but we did once in spite of that," he said, throwing his arm around my shoulder. "We're buddies, ain't we? Just you wait."

And another time, realizing that he preferred partners in their mid-twenties: "Am I too old, Mike? Have I become a father-image for you?"

"Nah," he said. "And that's a damned good thing, too. My pop used to whale the daylights outa me, and cuff me around all over the place. Good thing you don't remind me of him; I guess I wouldn't ever see you again." He looked thoughtful. "Or would I? I dunno."

He untwisted himself from my three-legged stool and stood up and stretched. Then he laughed. "Father-image! That's a good one, Daddy-o."

It was difficult for me to realize the astonishingly provocative nature of the way I acted towards Mike. It is a wonder he did not abandon me entirely.

I suffered acutely, interpreting every casual word and gesture of his as something relating especially to me, and not seeing at the moment how clouded my thinking was. He would wink carelessly at me over a cigarette, and my heart would pound. "What does he mean by that? Does he mean tonight?" I would think, but of course he meant nothing at all.

It was the sad little affair of Frankie Rogers, however, that pulled me up short. The kid had come to town with one of the musicals currently showing, and he wrote me a note, having got my address from a mutual friend. Then he came to call. He was a kind of pleasant empty-faced Broadway boy, with bleached blond hair and a wide mouth. Since I knew my friend's tastes, I asked Frankie what his were.

"Same as Hal's" he said, and smiled.

"How would you like me to introduce you to a charming fellow—very accomplished musician—some evening?"

Frankie moistened his lips. "Love it," he said.

So that evening I called Mike. I was so sunken in my infatuation that I did not see what I was doing until the beast that was my tongue had broken loose, and then there was no way to recapture it. "Tell you something," I prattled on to Mike blithely, "I'll introduce you to a new feller if you'll see me Monday night."

The pause over the phone should have warned me. At last Mike said—quite snappish and at the same time bored, if the two can be brought together: "Lissen, don't try to make bargains like that. I might not feel like it Monday. I'll set the dates, see? I just don't operate like that."

The voice came all the way from the Arctic. And the sudden realization of just what I had done chilled me as much as the voice. To have engaged in a transaction, a trade, a barter deal like that! All the way home that night I repeated over and over to myself, "Just what the hell has happened to me?" I felt low and mean and dirty.

It was at that point that I, feeling like a fly caught in tanglefoot,

69

made a definite effort to escape. I tried to neutralize the pattern before it became permanent.

But nothing seemed to work. All my efforts to toughen the hide, to pull a shell up over the emotions, to stuff my heart back into its old and dented armor — all were failures.

At what point in such a relationship is the breakpoint reached? I felt that it was close. Mike looked at me intently one day in the shop.

"Just what's the matter with you?" he said. "What's eatin' you? You ain't been yourself for a coupla weeks."

"I'm in love," I snapped.

Mike's eyebrows rose. "Izzat so?" he said. "Who with?"

"Oh, lord," I said in exasperation. "You don't know him."

Mike looked quizzical, and stuck his tongue in his cheek. "You know, you *do* remind me of my old man, much as I remember of him. He'd get moody the way you do, and then he'd snarl at everybody. Or give me a real whopping."

"Too bad he couldn't have beat some empathy into you," I said. "It's what you lack most."

"What's empathy?" said Mike innocently.

At that moment Dave came into the shop, and we stopped being nasty to each other. Dave had that knack: he smoothed the troubled waters. He talked about a new chair he was going to buy for the house, and then finally he said, "Well, I guess we can't go to a drive-in this Sunday. I've got to go to a recital, and you'll have to spend the evening with Mike."

My heart began to pound. I was sure this was it. Mike's face showed neither irritation nor pleasure. He asked who was playing, and that was all.

That was Wednesday, and I thought Sunday would never come. But it did. There had been no word all day from either of them. Then at seven-thirty Mike came in. He had on his full uniform again — jacket and boots and freshly laundered army fatigues with the side pockets — and his skin was dark from having evidently been in the sun all day.

He sat down. "Well," he said. "I gotta go to the recital after all. Dave insists."

My disappointment didn't show itself in so much as a flicker of an eye, or the twitch of a muscle in my cheek. "Well, you'd better get goin' then," I said, looking at the clock, "or you'll be late, if you've gotta change clothes."

Mike shrugged. "I don't care if I am late," he said. "Dave tried to get three tickets, but they were all sold out. I'm sorry."

He hung around until twenty minutes to eight. If the thing started promptly, he'd be very late. He explained once again, and then he finally left. I stared at the wall.

There was too much that didn't hang together. Dave could never have got him near a piano recital. Somehow, another ticket could have been procured. Mike had had the hunter's look glinting in his eye; I knew it too well. No, the little things added up to the large one: Mike wanted to go out by himself that evening, and not spend it with me . . .

So, after he left, I went out alone. I went across the bay, to all the old and evil spots I used to know while I had been drinking. But I didn't drink that night. I wandered, I enjoyed my sadness. And then I went home alone, having avoided all the spots where Mike might have been.

Somehow the air seemed poisoned after that. I could no longer think of anything much to say when I was with them, and they too became more quiet. I feared that our friendship was headed for the rocks, and from the deeps of my self-pity I blamed them.

The uneasiness between us went on for a couple of weeks. Then one evening Mike came into the shop and sat down. "You know what?" he said, almost belligerently. "I want me a tattoodle, daddy-o."

Nothing surprised me any longer. The elusive thumbscrew had dropped right into my lap. "Okay, sonny boy," I said, "what'll it be? You sure you want this? They're kinda permanent, you know."

"Yup," he said, with conviction. "I figger I could use some Navy design, since I been in the Merchant Marine. That's close enough, ain't it?"

I shrugged. "No law says you gotta be a sailor to have an anchor," I said.

Mike looked at the Navy designs, and finally picked out an anchor with an eagle, and some flowers sprinkled here and there — a good design for a long-boned forearm, which he had. He fitted the stencil to his skin, then looked up. "Haven't you got another outfit at home?" he said.

I nodded. "Yeah, my traveling case."

"How's about us goin' there and puttin' it on at your place?" he said. "Instead of here?" He grinned. "Could have a drink, too."

"All right," I said. It was a lot more comfortable, and not much more trouble. On the way, Mike was strangely quiet. "What's the matter?" I asked once. "Scared?"

He looked over from his corner of the taxi. "First time," he said.

"Nothing to it," I said.

But I knew something Mike didn't know, a difficult thing to explain. I'd seen it happen thousands of times. With the first setting of the needle into the skin, a whole new relationship unfolded between my customers and myself. I became for them—almost mystically—their best boyfriend, father confessor, mother, buddy in their gang—everything. Countless times, young hoods had told me all their heartaches and fears, things I'm sure they had never told another living being. I found myself wondering how it would hit Mike.

When we got to my house on Filbert (what a name for a street!), I busied myself with the equipment. "Make yourself a drink," I told Mike, and he did. But he watched me nervously. I plugged in the power pack, stirred up the inks, got out the alcohol and antiseptics, took the protective grease-coat off the machines, tested the needles, and then looked up at him. His face was more pale than usual. It dawned on me that these preparations were as frightening as the assorted clankings, cracks and thuddings that Mike liked so much to make in his music room. I gave several nasty little test buzzes on my needle.

"All right, sonny," I said. "Come sit here."

He was acutely nervous. "Does it really hurt much?" he asked.

"Kind of a burning sensation," I said. I was enjoying this. "The outliner hurts worse than the shader. Pity we have to use it first."

Mike took a long drink. "I—dunno—," he began nervously, then set his glass down.

"Ah, c'mon!" I scoffed. "You, the big tough guy who can dish it out—and can't take it, huh?"

"I hate needles," Mike said, wetting his lips again.

I shaved his forearm, sterilized it, put a thin bit of vaseline on it, and pressed the outline of the stencil against his skin. He was trembling, and quite tense.

72

I poked his deltoid. "You gotta relax up here," I said. "You're all tight, and that'll make me screw up the lines."

He let out a big breath, and tried to relax. "Okay," he said, and I began.

He fought me with deep muscular tension all through the outline. And then I saw him begin to show the signs of shock: he drew two deep ragged breaths, and with his free hand fiddled a bit at the back of his neck. I felt the skin begin to grow a shade cooler. But I did nothing. With anyone else, I would have stopped at the first sign, bent his head down between his knees and applied pressure — to force the blood back to his noggin. I would have given him a sip of water and let him lie down for five minutes, and he would have been over it.

But I let Mike go, deliberately. I heard his breathing grow more shallow. I went on working and he watched me — the worst thing he could have done. And finally, quietly and with no fuss, he rolled gently off the chair. I was ready for him; I caught him and eased him to the floor and stayed on my knees beside him. His breathing was still shallow; the sweat was heavy on his forehead. And suddenly he began to shake, and then strain; I knew consciousness was about four seconds away, and I raised my hand. When his eyelids flickered, I slapped him hard, once on each cheek. I enjoyed doing it.

It jarred him. He groaned.

I slapped his cheeks again. "Can't take it, huh?" I jeered.

Suddenly, unexpectedly, he raised on one elbow and then threw his arms around my waist. He buried his head in the slanting lap my position gave me. "D-dad," he said in a muffled voice, "don't hit me any more."

I lifted his head from my lap by his hair, and stared for a full minute at his face. He could not look into my eyes; the lids lowered and he tried to turn aside. I knew then that he was mine to do with what I liked. I pushed him away so that he rolled over once on the floor. He lay there face down. He was weeping, great dry sobs.

I looked down at him, but I did not see him. Instead, my eyes looked through him into the deep pit of my obsession, and saw the broken image lying at the bottom. And then, almost as in a trance, I saw the pit begin to fill with the moving waters of pity, flowing in and drowning the shattered image that lay there.

73

And yet, I felt strangely grateful to him. The detour that I had taken had been the wrong one, but it had shown me that I was still capable of love.

I tested my breathing. It went evenly and smoothly. I had regained my freedom, and life was — once again — stretching its broad path out ahead of me. And then I reached over, and shook him by the shoulder, and gave him a comradely thump. "Buck up, old boy," I said. "Everything is quite all right."

The Tattooed Harpist

Two hours after midnight in New York City on 10th Avenue in the Fifties. There's a perfect recipe for a scary neighborhood.

There are long stretches of blackness as the streets head up a little incline away from the river, and then occasionally a small dim yellow puddle of worthless light under an old-fashioned street lamp. There was hardly anyone on the sidewalks—probably all in bed, or quivering behind their closed steel shutters with loaded shotgun. And if you did meet anyone on these streets, he was bound to look tougher than hell—turtleneck sweaters, leather jackets. Mean, man.

Of course I was dressed just as tough as they were, in my uniform—and even had my jolly stompers on, my black heavy boots. It had been a lousy evening—no scores, no johns, and Times Square deader than a whorehouse on Sunday morning. I'd made the rounds—the Hotel Markwell bar, 42nd Street, Kelly's, and the rest. A few punk kids, no more. And it was chilly—a little snow hanging around the edges, as you expect it to be in February in Manhattan. And I was horny, hornier than a stag at eve, and wanted a man—even if I had to take him for free.

I rounded the corner off 10th Avenue into my street, and stopped dead in my tracks. There was a six-foot-tall stud standing just outside the circle of light from a street lamp. He was all in black leather—cap, jacket, boots, even leather trousers. But what shocked me was he had his fly open and a good firm hold on himself, thumb underneath and four fingers curled over the top, and he was really beatin' it. I had a sort of flash thought about Lili Marlene standing underneath the street lamp—but a Lili who was a male and all in leather to boot, and with no need to be afflicted with envy or sorrow of any kind.

"Sheez!" I said, drawing my breath in. He looked over at me but didn't stop. His right jacket cuff was unzipped and turned back, and his black sweater pulled up. A new tattoo glistened with a blood-sheen on his right forearm, the one he was working with.

"You want it, man?" he said, sort of tense and hard.

"Not here, dammit," I said. I stood and watched him, then looked around. There was no one in sight, but this was too dangerous for me. "Ain'tcha got no place we can go?" I asked.

He slowed down his work a little, thought it over, and then stuck his cock away. "Sure," he said. "I live up the street a ways. Wanta come along?"

I looked him up and down. He wasn't too big for me to handle, I reckoned; and I could hold my own if he started anything. A pretty even match.

"What's your name?" he said.

"Duke Andrews," I said. I was still jumpy about leaving Chicago so fast, with that young gangster Luigi di Lupo on my tail, and so I was using another name.

"Dave Metcalf," he said. We didn't shake hands.

We kept walking up the crosstown street I lived on but I didn't say anything. Not knowing much about New York I'd taken the first apartment I could find, there in the West Fifties. It had the facade of an old building, one of the salvaged ones. They had scooped out all the inside wooden guts of it and poured nice cement floors and staircases and ceilings, so that in certain weathers the place sweated like an underground tomb. You'd expect the building to be full of dockhands and construction workers and longshoremen, as close to the river as it was—but not so. Instead it was filled with frilly secretaries, both male and female, and old maids of both sexes, the kind that retired at ten and got up at six. You hardly ever saw anyone in the halls. And damned if one Saturday morning before I got out of bed I hadn't even heard some cunt practicing a harp somewhere on the floor below me! It sure would be a gasser if this new stud lived in the same building.

76

"Kinda dangerous pastime for you back there," I said while we loped along. I think each of us was trying to outstep the other, which made us seem to be in a great hurry.

He made a deep sound in his throat. "Yeah," he said. "But a new tattoo always gets me hotter than hell. And there was nobody around except me."

"I know what you mean," I said. I remembered how I'd stood in front of a mirror, naked, when I got that dickybird on my shoulder in Chicago, and what had happened to me, feeling as burly and dominant and male as I did. I couldn't keep my hands off myself. "I thought tattoos were illegal in New York City."

He rocked his hand sidewise in front of him. "They sure are," he said. "No shops open, but some are sneakin' it. I was at a private party this afternoon where they'd flown a tattoodler in from Chicago . . ."

I stiffened. "Not by any chance ole Pete Swallow?" I asked.

He looked at me oddly. "Yeah," he said. "The same. Why—you got some of his work?"

I put my hand on my shoulder, on the jacket. "Yeah," I said.

"Damn," he said. We rushed on through the night, two dinosaurs heading for our mating ground.

Sure enough, we lived in the same building. He unlocked the door and I turned my face down so he wouldn't see the grin I was trying to control. They always say your own backyard is the one that has the diamonds in it.

I got my first good look at him when we stepped into the hallway. He had a lean tanned face—probably sunlamped—but full of interesting planes and high cheekbones and cleft chins and suchlike, all conventionally put together and pleasing enough, but with just some little extra touch that kept him from being one of those TV beauties that usually are so full of complexes they can't even get hard. I finally saw what it was . . . one eye had a very small cast in it, making him squint. It was hardly enough to notice, and yet it wouldn't let you stop looking at his face until you could identify what it was that kept dragging your glance back to him. And there was a small jagged blue scar running down one side of his chin—very faint, the sort you get when a motorcycle throws you into a pile of cinders and gravel.

"You ride a bike?" I asked, as I went up the stairs behind him. I said it low and walked easy; it was late.

"I did," he said. "but there was a bad accident and I quit."

"Your chin?" I asked.

"Yeah," he said. "And eye."

He lived on the second floor right directly under my apartment. I got so tickled I chuckled a little and then had to try to hide it with a cough. He stopped at the door and unlocked it. "G'wan in," he said. "Not much, but it'll do."

It was just like my place—neat and clean and cold, cupboards and shelves and a double bed. A room divider, a small stove area, a tiny bathroom—and then the living room. I turned to look at it and damn near fell through the cement floor. There—big and golden and seeming twice as large because of the smallness of the apartment—stood a huge glittering concert-sized harp, dripping with goldleaf grapes and baroque scrolls and rococo garbage.

I gulped. "Goddlemighty," I said.

"Yeah," he said. "Most everybody is surprised. And also, I work on Wall Street."

"You mean you are a regular leather-wearin' card-carryin' motorcyclist and also play the harp?" I asked, astonished. "Or you just a B & B leatherboy?"

"B & B?" he frowned. "What's that?"

"Bosh & Bullshit," I said. "A pseudosadist or pseudo-m."

He shook his head. "I don't know if I'm the real McCoy," he said.

"Who does?" I said.

He was taking his jacket off. "I can try to show you if you want," he said, sort of hard. He pulled the black turtleneck Navy sweater up over his head. He had one of those lean rangy bodies—and four big tattoos on his arms, and an eagle with spread wings on his chest. The new tattoo on his forearm was a fine green and red dragon.

I started to undress myself. "Nah," I said. "No need to. I just like sex, not fighting. Besides, it's too late to fight." I grinned at him.

He grinned back. "Bed or floor?" he said.

I looked at the rough raffia carpeting. I kind of understood how he felt, with his new tattoo and the consciousness of it rampaging through his blood like some uncontrolled and fatal fever—and creating inside him the necessity to be the Hero, if only for one

78

night. Damn, but some men today are sure mixed up!

"Floor," I said, and when I was naked lay down flat on it, looking up.

After he had peeled off his leather pants he put his motorcycle boots back on, and fastened a black leather belt around his middle. Then he produced a padlock from somewhere and carefully closed it around the small neck of flesh just above his kumquats. And then he straddled me and began to speak.

It's hard for me to believe that a Wall Street harpist could talk dirtier than I could, for I learned my dirty talk in the best schools in the world—docks, whorehouses, hotels—and in driving trucks and taxicabs. Yet here was a mere harp-player, a Brooks brother who worked in a broker's office, easily pushing me off the edge. I never in my life heard a steadier stream of insults, delivered in a low insistent steely voice, with the bottom of his boot scraping across my chest for punctuation. For variety, he would step back to his first position with a foot to each side of my rib cage, catching just enough flesh between the edge of the boots and the raffia carpeting to leave me bruised and yellow-blue for days.

You could look through all the laws of every State in the Union and not find one that we broke that night. There was not even a single one of the "contacts" for which you can get twenty years. Instead, I suppose you might call it preadolescent play, the kind of early biological experimenting that goes on between small boys behind barns. From my prone position (and it was amazing to me how easily I took the passive role!) Dave appeared tremendous. He was ten feet tall, and the rangy lithe form went up and up into the gloom, while all the time his hand was busy with himself. And as his tension increased and the moment arrived, his voice became more and more excited, his words more and more filthy, until in a sudden burst he exploded like a skyrocket filled with hot snow. I joined him before the fallout was done. Then doubled over, gasping, he brought his boot back to my chest and smeared its bottom slowly up and down my torso.

Afterwards I took a quick shower and said goodbye, with a handshake.

Dave stuck his head and shoulder around the edge of the door as I left. "See you around sometime," he said.

"Yeah, man," I said, grinning. And then instead of going down the stairs, I started up them to my room.

His mouth opened from shock and his eyes widened.

"You can just bet you'll see me, buddy," I said, "since I live right over you." And I flicked my finger against my cap brim as I vanished around the landing.

Anyone who has ever tried to break himself into a new city — or break a city to him — knows that the first weeks are difficult. You miss a friend or companion most of all, some buddy to chew the fat with. Dave was that for me. I had got me a job on the docks for the time being, and when I came home dirty and tired it was very enjoyable to take a shower and then go down and chin with Dave, or go out with him to get something to eat. Occasionally we cooked up a gah-damned mess of some sort in his apartment or mine. I think neither of us would ever have taken any awards from the Escoffier Society. I didn't think we would have wanted to. Male cooks were just a leetle suspect in our all too utterly utter masculine world . . .

We talked about everything under the sun, as new friends will. Dave had a good mind. He'd almost finished a master's degree in — of all things — Greek and Latin at the University of Minnesota. And he hated his mother.

"Gah-damned bitch," he said. "Talk about your silver cord. Not umbilical for me — I was really wrapped up in one, trussed like a steer for branding. And branded . . . 'M'. 'M' is for the many things you gave me, Mother dear . . . You know," he said, "while I was under her domination I used to stammer so bad you couldn't understand me?"

"I don't hear any of it now."

Dave leaned back and took a drink of his coke. He didn't drink alcohol and he didn't smoke — thought too much of his body to ruin it those ways. "No," he said, "and I owe it all to Doctor Bill in Chicago. He — "

"You don't mean Bill Broderick, by any chance?" I said.

Dave leaned forward. "Sure!" he said. "You know him too?"

I waggled my hand. "Made the scene a few times," I said uncomfortably. I hoped there was no communication between them. "You hear from him much?"

"I never hear," Dave said. "And I never write. But he got hold of

80

me one night and we had some pizza and coke at my place, and he talked to me for hours about the Great Bitch All-Mother and how you had to break free at some point in your life."

"Do you any good?" I asked.

"The next morning I'd stopped stammering," Dave said. "I never stuttered again."

"A cure or just a temporary arrest?" I said. "I'm suspicous of such quick recoveries."

Dave shrugged. "I dunno," he said. "But three weeks later I sold my motorcycle—hadn't been on it since the accident—and packed my books and my harp and came to New York. And I haven't talked since to the old bitch or answered her letters—yeah, she finally located my address through the phone company. But it's all over."

"Dead—or just buried?" I persisted. "It may fester."

Dave shook his head. "I think it's dead."

There was a soft knock at his door. I straightened up a little and looked down at myself, but everything was in order. "Who's that?" I said, low.

Dave raised a shoulder. "Maybe Carol," he said. He got up and went to the door and opened it.

"Hi!" came a girl's voice. "Can I borrow some sugar?"

"Sure," said Dave. "Come in." He opened the door. I was conscious of a tightening up inside me, and a kind of chilling—my usual reaction for the past few years since I gave up trying to be a hetero.

"This is Duke," he said. "Carol."

"Hello," I said. I didn't get up. She was a sort of black-haired girl, secretary-type. She had the usual number of eyes and legs and arms and boobs. I couldn't have cared less. She sensed it.

Dave got her the sugar and she said goodbye and left. When he closed the door I said, "She's after you . . . Sugar!"

"Maybe," he said.

"What is she—one of those freak girls who can't make out with real men so they play around with all the queers?"

"I don't really know," Dave said. He looked uneasy.

"You ever been to bed with a woman?" I asked.

Dave looked down. "Nope," he said. "I'd kinda like to try it."

"Don't bother," I said. "Too loose. You get the same effect with a pound of warm liver. Does she know about you?"

He nodded. "Yes," he said.

"And so she thinks that all you need is the love of a good pure woman to turn you into a nice tame hetero hubby for suburbia, huh?"

"She hasn't really made a play for me," Dave said. He was getting a little red in the face.

"Well, take it from me, buddy boy—leave the cunts alone," I said. "Your pattern is already set. You go tryin' to screw around with it and you're likely to end up in the loony bin. You're too delicately balanced as it is. Harp and motorcycle and tattoos—to gain attention. Mother cut out and rejected. A quick cure on your stuttering. Carol might be just what you need to send you off the deep end permanently."

Dave grinned. "I'll certainly consider what you said, Doctor Andrews. How much do I owe you for the evening's consultation?"

I stretched mightily with my hands above my head and stuck my legs out in front of my chair. "Oh, I don't rightly know," I said. "How about just a small blowjob?"

So that's the way it was between Dave and me—just lots of good fellowship and camaraderie.

March gave way to April and the park spruced itself up and the trees began to bud and all the sap started to flow, in people just the same as bushes. I got a promotion and a raise of a buck an hour, and that with what I got from hustling on the side kept me pretty well off. I didn't like the dock work especially, because it was so damned hard; but on the other hand I realized it kept me in good physical shape so that I didn't have to go to a gym or do exercises— which I hated.

I was sailing along then pretty fine, but Dave was acting a little peculiar. He had been very amiable at first and always ready with a joke; and then as the weeks went by I began to notice he was silent a good deal of the time, and sort of melancholy. It all came to a head in May.

I had just got home and finished my shower when Dave knocked on the door—his regular knock, three shorts and a long. "C'mon in!" I hollered, toweling myself between the legs and then bending over to dry my feet.

When I straightened up I was shocked. Dave was standing at

the bathroom door. His usually tanned face was grey, the kind of ugly shade skin gets when it turns white under tan, and his mouth was squared away in a kind of fish-mouth and he was trying to talk. But nothing came out—just the gasping and choking.

"Hey!" I yelled. I dropped the towel and grabbed him by the arm. "Take it easy, man," I said. "Come on in the front room and sit down and tell me all about it."

When I said that he collapsed—just wilted, and his knees sagged so that I was sort of holding him in my arms, with his body sliding down my body. I thought at first he'd fainted, except that he was too rigid for fainting. Then I thought of a lot of other things too, like strokes and epilepsy and grand mal and petit mal and psychomotor attacks, and it all scared the hell out of me.

I managed to drag him into the front room and hoist him up on the bed. He had only a T-shirt and trousers on, so I loosened his belt. Then I got a cold wet towel from the sink and slapped it on his forehead and eyes. I'm not much for first aid, I guess. I didn't know whether to give him a shot of whiskey or a tranquilizer, but then I remembered he didn't drink and this was perhaps not the best moment to start. So I got the tranquilizers and gave him two, enough to knock you into a state of suspended animation for six hours, I figured, if you were healthy. It ought to calm him down somewhat, at least.

About a half hour later he showed signs of improving. His hands were still cold and wet, but the trembling had stopped.

"Dave," I said, "what happened? Can you tell me?"

Well, it was a fearful thing to listen to—that effort to talk. I never heard so much choking and stammering in my life. It was painful as hell to me. Sometimes he couldn't get a word out at all, and had to leave it and find another. But what I finally made out was this:

He'd been off work that Friday afternoon, and so had Carol—and she came over and tried to make him. They had undressed and gone to bed and then his apparatus had failed him, utterly and completely. And Carol, instead of trying to help, had laughed at him and taunted him and called him all sorts of things. Finally she dressed and left, and Dave passed out for an hour or so. Then he came around and managed to make it up to see me.

I said a few choice things about Carol but I was really thinking about what I should do. How do you treat a rattlesnake bite on the psyche? It called for swift strong measures, and I didn't know what they were. Food? Naw—and besides I didn't want to leave him alone while I went out for some. Of course I could have used that old pair of Navy leg irons on him and locked him away from the knives and poisons and razor blades, but something told me I ought to think of some more dramatic remedy or distraction, even though temporary. I didn't have any psychiatrist friends in New York.

So I used logic—or maybe only commonsense, the only weapon available to me to bring down the strange winged terrors which were battering the grey valleys of his brain. I sat down, still naked, on the floor beside the bed, and pulled him over on his side to face me.

"Dave," I said, shaking him. He opened his eyes and I wished he'd left them shut. They were red and tortured.

"Dave," I said again, low. "Spit in my face."

It didn't register. I said it again. The second time it did. His eyes widened a little, in shock. I shut my own eyes and turned my face upwards. "Go on," I said. "Spit."

I felt him raise up a little and then I felt it land—violently, spattering all over my forehead and cheeks. It was all I could do to keep from raising my hand to wipe it away.

"Do it again," I said, opening my mouth. "In here this time." I shut my eyes again and felt it hit the back of my throat. I swallowed. It was awful, but I had to help him rebuild himself from the shattered and crumbled masonry of his ego. And then on my knees I crawled to the foot of the bed. I yanked off the loafer on his right foot. He had no socks on. I kissed his foot and toes, all the time watching him for reactions. His eyes were closed again; his chest arched. He grabbed the covers with tight clawed hands.

I took my mouth off his foot and reached up and grabbed his trousers and pulled them off. He didn't raise his legs to help me. Then I swung around to the side of the bed and put my face close to his.

"Dave," I said, low and intense. "Please come and stand over me."

I lay down flat on the floor. I didn't know if it would work. I was trembling a little myself by now. And I could hardly force myself to say what I knew I'd have to say. I never used the word any more. It didn't exist in a hustler's world. Yet I knew I would have to speak it.

"D-Dave," I said. "Come on, Dave. I—I-love you. Come on, Davey. I'm yours. Please. Do what you want to with me. I'm all yours, Davey. I—l-love you."

The word almost choked in my throat. I said it several times, and each time it came out with an extra "l" in front of it. I was the one stammering now. But I went on talking, very low key.

"P-please, Davey—I'm your s-slave. I love you. I love you." Finally it was not as hard to say as it had been. And then suddenly I saw a long lean leg slipping over the side of the bed, and the other one followed it. He stood up, his hand in the same position as the first time I had ever seen him. He was excited again, and scowling. He put one foot on each side of my rib cage.

"You bastard," he said, very clear and distinctly. "I'll show you. This time you're gonna take it and go on begging for more." There was no sign of a stammer anywhere.

And leaning over me he opened his mouth and let a long slow stream of spittle fall directly toward my face. Somehow I knew that I must not turn aside, that I had to take it with open eyes.

Well, that was that. Dave seemed all right for the next few weeks. But it was now myself who had changed. I was as embarrassed as hell to be with him, after that "confession" of "love." And I was a little frightened too. It seemed to me that his psyche must be like an old inner tube, patched over and over, with patches on the patches. How long it would last without blowing completely was anyone's guess.

So it made me nervous to be around him. And for that reason I began to look for another place to stay. I finally found a small apartment down in the Village on MacDougal Street, and one Sunday—when I thought he had gone to the country with friends—I just packed my few belongings and moved down there. I said nothing to him about it, and left no forwarding address. It's easy to lose yourself in New York. Lots of people do, even when they know their way around, like Dave. Or like me.

But there was one funny little twist to all of it. I went back a month later to pick up my mail, which I had asked the landlord to keep for me until I got settled. He gave me a packet of about six letters. And then he held up another bunch also tied with string.

"Do you want to take Metcalf's to him?" he said.

I was surprised. "Doesn't he live here any more?"

It was the landlord's turn to raise his eyebrows. "Isn't he with you?" he asked. "I thought you moved out to live together. I thought that's what he said. You left on a Sunday afternoon; he left in the evening."

I could hardly think of an answer. "Er . . . he'll probably call for them himself," I said, and left a little confused. And vaguely annoyed.

Evidently we had both felt the same about his "cure," and about that last painful scene. But it was certainly not very comradely of him to say nothing to me about his plans.

I may just stop in at a harp recital sometime and ask him why he didn't. In my full hustler's uniform, of course. He's sure to be there.

The Cuba Caper

It was the third time the steward on the Air France liner to Havana from Paris had dropped something in the aisle—first a plastic cup, then a plastic plate, and this time a paper napkin.

After the plate fell, and I saw the quick darting look as he bent down to try to see up under my kilt, I readjusted the sporran so that it no longer nestled between my legs, and tightened the hem of the proud plaid kilt so that the next time he would be able to gratify his little French heart.

When he bent to pick up the napkin, I watched his eyes. They traveled up under the kilt, widened as I arched my hips forward a little, and then his mouth opened. He ran the tip of his tongue over the edge of his upper lip, and finally thought to look me in the face. I was grinning.

I winked at him. He spoke at once. "Monsieur wishes something?"

I looked over at the dowager next to the window. She was sound asleep. "Och," I said in my best Scot's accent. "Ye're a bra' lad. 'Tis summat ye wanted yersel', no?"

He blushed deep red. "J-just to see if Monsieur ... if Monsieur ..."

". . . wore summat beneath the kilt?" I looked at my watch. "I'll be for using the men's room in fifteen minutes," I said. "The one aft the starboard side."

"I will prepare it for Monsieur," he said in a low voice, and got up from his knees to go towards the rear of the plane.

What a crazy world it was! Here I was—at the expense of the United States State Department—on the way to Havana with a Scottish passport, a full set of carefully forged credentials, three different complete Scots outfits with kilts, and with a dirty little plan so carefully rehearsed into me that I could not have forgotten it if I tried.

They fired me from the State Department in Washington three years before, because they caught me in the men's room with another guy, pants down, having a high old time. So I went on to other pursuits. Two months ago I had been called back to Washington by my former boss.

I was shown directly into his office when I got there. He motioned me to a seat. His hair was a little greyer, and as carefully combed as ever. I had long suspected him of being a club member himself, but a little more discreet than I had been.

"Sit down, Jock," he said. "You're Scottish, aren't you?"

I motioned to my dossier spread open before him. "You can see that yourself, Mr. Brent," I said. "Perhaps you'll be able to tell me why you took me away from my current job and brought me here, after firing me three years ago."

"A matter of patriotism, Jack," he said. "We want you to do something for us."

I shrugged. "You think for one moment I will?" I said sarcastically. "After the treatment I got here?"

He sighed. "A lot has happened since then," he said, a little wearily. "We apologize for it all. We've changed our way of thinking. You admitted you were a homosexual—"

"—along with several million others," I said bitterly, "both in and out of the State Department."

"Yes, I know," he said. "Well, here it is—and you don't have to accept. But we know you're a Scot, that you speak Spanish fluently and perfectly. We want to send you to Edinburgh for three weeks to pick up the Scots accent again. Then we want you to go to Havana, all expenses paid, as a tourist—in full McAndrews kilt and tartan."

I was astounded. "Whatever for?"

Mr. Brent smiled. He wasn't a bad-looking old duffer when he did. "Bait," he said. "Here's the way it is. The Big Boss down in Cuba has got at least one homo on his staff, a fellow they call

'Pipon' Fajardo—*Pipon* means potbelly, I think—who's filling the boss's ear with stronger anti-U.S. policies than ever before. We want you to get involved with Pipon, and then one of our undercover agents will photograph him in the act of . . . er . . . doing something to you which will discredit him."

"You mean," I said, "you want him to be photographed blowing me?"

A pained look appeared in Mr. Brent's eyes. "Well, er . . . yes . . . I guess that's the expression."

I laughed. "So there is a use for the gay boys after all," I said bitterly.

"You have to fight fire with fire sometimes," Mr. Brent murmured.

So here I was. The stay in Edinburgh had been fun, and accustoming myself to the kilt even more of a lark. I picked up the accent again quickly, having long ago heard it from my grandfather. The strong scarlets and greens of the McAndrews clan were mine to wear openly. The great black-trimmed white-furred sporran, with the pocket on the inside, dangled between my legs, and the air blew free beneath my kilt. The 'trainer' in Edinburgh had explained that I could wear small black briefs if I wanted to, but that the military never did. He even laughingly explained that a Scots soldier, leaving his barracks for a night on the town, had to pause over a mirror set in the floor, so that an inspector could check to see that he had nothing on. " 'Tis good for the health of the body," the trainer laughed, "to leave 'em danglin' free, and 'tis a mighty come-on to all the bra' lads and lassies."

I surveyed the situation. "But there's naught to hold it down," I said. " 'Tis na' richt to get excited, then."

"Na, 'tis not," said old Mac. " 'Tis an exercise in control to keep it fra' stickin' out and pushin' the sporran skywards."

A great old guy. I liked him. "Ye'll be havin' no secret weapons on ye," he explained. " 'Tis by order." And then a sly grin came over his wrinkled face. "But havin' seen what hangs betwixt your bra' legs, me lad," he said, " 'tis my guess ye'll need none other."

And that was all I had—my camera, guidebook, my oversize secret weapon—not even a cyanide pill in case I was caught. And part of my instruction was to pretend to know no Spanish at all, but to listen with a large ear . . .

I felt a brush on my arm. The handsome little black-haired steward was going down the aisle. I turned in my seat to watch him. He went into the starboard toilet, so I rose and walked back toward the johns. There was no one else waiting to get in; the closest stewardess was bending over a passenger at the middle of the plane, talking.

I eased open the door and went in, my tam-o'-shanter set at a rakish angle. The steward was making himself very thin behind the door. He shut and bolted it quickly.

"Monsieur does . . . not mind?" he whispered.

"Mind what?" I said, playing stupid.

His hot slender hand stole down towards the sporran and pushed it aside. I felt his fingers on my secret weapon through the cloth, and made no move to back away. It would have been useless anyway—my butt was resting against the wall. I looked in the mirror above the washbowl, and sighed. This damned kilt outfit brought out all my narcissism. In the mirror was a handsome guy, six feet two, with dark chestnut hair just touched here and there with a glint of copper, a white skin, and a pretty damned good face—staring back at me.

The little French steward suddenly disappeared below the angle of the mirror, and all I could see was myself. But then suddenly my sporran rose into the mirror's reflection, and started to move slowly up and down. And somewhere beneath the light sexual touch of the wool I felt the hot mouth of the little steward exploring, his tongue darting around the bush of hair, then swallowing first one kumquat and then the other—but oh, so gently!—and finally moving on to the main attraction. Under the ministration of his hot talented tongue and lips I soon felt myself rising skyward, even beyond our altitude of thirty-five thousand feet; I reached out to grip the underside of the washbasin to hold myself down. And then I began to feel the heat of comets sliding down my spine, and suddenly the sun went nova and exploded in a burst of brilliance behind my tight-clenched eyelids . . .

The face appeared from underneath my kilt, flushed, the hair mussed. I looked down into his sparkling eyes and smiled. He smiled at me.

"M-monsieur," he said, a little out of breath; "Monsieur . . . is quite a man! M-monsieur will possibly be the most popular *tour-*

iste to arrive in la Cuba for the past year . . ."

I grinned at him and ruffled his hair with my hand.

"*Merci infiniment,*" I said to him.

He looked at his watch. "Eet took us only a hundred and twenty miles, air-time," he said.

I laughed.

"Where will Monsieur be staying in Havana?"

"The Hotel Parado."

He nodded. "There is a very . . . how you say? . . . *sympathique* bar in that hotel. I will be there again on Friday; eet is now Monday. May I see Monsieur there at nine of the Friday evening?"

I ruffled his hair again. "Of course," I said, "if I can arrange it. And your name is . . .?

"Marcel," he said. "Marcel Gagnon."

I stuck out my hand. "Jock McAndrews," I said, giving him my best sexy smile.

He opened the edge of the door a little and looked out. "All is safe," he said, and disappeared.

I looked down at myself. My damned secret weapon was not so secret; it pushed the sporran too far forward. I would have to wait a couple of minutes. So I folded my arms, rested my butt on the washbowl, and thought about the starving Armenians.

I guess the stay in Cuba would be sort of fun after all, if this beginning was any indication of the way things would go.

But a hundred and twenty miles air-time, indeed! I'd have to do better than that. A hundred ought to have been the limit. I'd have to get back in shape for all those handsome tawny Latin lovers . . . and ole Pipon.

The plane slid in to a very smooth landing at Havana airport. It looked fairly modern and prosperous, like any other big airport: lots of glass windows from floor to ceiling. There was only one difference; they hadn't been washed in years, evidently.

We followed the stewardess in a sheeplike line to the customs house. She was, or could have been, an attractive woman; but the regime had decreed no lipstick or rouge and she looked rather colorless, despite her dark-toned skin. In such cases, it's the males who look better: they always have the red-bronze on the cheeks, and their lips are dark and inviting.

My luck took me to a customs official who was small, dark, tawny, and exciting looking. He had big black eyes, and the way they darted here and there indicated that he was a club member, despite the ruling that Uncle Fidel had made that there was to be no homosexuality in Cuba. I saw him swallow hard, twice, at the sight of me in my kilt. The basket he carried looked gratifyingly full of goodies.

"Has the Señor anything to declare?" he asked me in English when my turn came.

"Nothing but myself," I said, giving him my biggest grin.

He seemed to be very nervous. "No matches, cigarettes, or liquor?" he asked.

I gulped. I had forgotten all about the few paper matchbooks I had brought from Edinburgh. "Er . . . no," I said, "except maybe I do have some matches. I didn't know. 'Tis na' richt?"

He shook his head so vigorously that even his curly hair moved. He was dressed in a very tight-fitting uniform, tighter — I noticed — than any of his fellow customs agents.

He looked very grave."Will the Señor open his suitcases?"

I did. There in one corner of the big one was a whole handful of matchbooks.

"The Señor will have to come with me," he said soberly. The smile was gone from his face, but the twinkle remained.

I closed my two bags and followed him away from the others, towards a door marked in Spanish: "Customs. Private."

When we were inside I put the bags on the floor. " 'Tis sorry I am," I said. "I dinna ken the rules."

He gestured vaguely. "We must inspect everything you have," he said. "You will please undress." He locked the door carefully.

It was a large bare room. There was a full-length mirror set against one wall. I looked at it momentarily, and saw that it had the darkish cast that two-way mirrors do, and I wondered who was on the other side.

I undressed, sneaking a look at myself in the mirror. I was not too displeased. Off came the kilt — and I thought I heard a smothered gasp from the handsome Cuban. I took off the sporran, the shoulder shawl, and the shirt, and soon stood there mother-naked, with not even the plaid stockings nor the black shoes on me. The only thing I left on was my tam-o'-shanter.

And then the small Cuban surprised me. With a deft movement he undid his belt. His fingers fumbled clumsily for a moment at the buttons of his fly, and his pants dropped to the floor. He opened a drawer in a desk and brought forth a tube of vaseline, which he put in the proper little brown spot. Then, smiling with even white teeth, he bent over a convenient railing. He turned and looked over his shoulder impishly. "We must offer the Señor from Scotland the full hospitality of our country."

I looked down at the two halves of the dark golden melon spread before me, and my secret weapon began to recharge itself, so that in a moment it was ready to fire. I noted the little dark rivulet of black hair running down the center of the halves. A real beauty he was, and come what may, I started on my journey into the celestial gate.

The entrance to paradise was about half-accomplished when he groaned a little, and as I grasped the two halves, spreading them fiercely apart, I felt the sweat spring out on the skin under my hands.

" 'Tis a bra' welcome ye gi' me," I said, pushing harder, "aye, that it is, but is't na' a bit daft?"

He muttered something I could not understand nor hear. But then I heard something else. Like a soft whirring flutter somewhere off in the distance, it reached my ear. And then I knew. It came from behind the two-way mirror. I was being photographed playing bum-tiddy-bum with the small customs officer.

Well, I thought, we'll give 'em a good show. And I redoubled my efforts, the movements growing wilder, bending my knees and hunching forward, then sidewise, grabbing him around the middle, and panting. It was not all faked, by any means. The kid knew how, and seemed to be enjoying it as much as I was. And then for the second time in twelve hours, my secret weapon fired itself.

I let my weight press down against him, knowing that the railing was almost cutting him in two in the middle. And so we rested for a moment.

Afterwards, I dressed again after washing off, and he pulled up his trousers. The soft whirring had stopped. I hope they got a good reel of that, I thought. Perhaps this guy is pimping here at customs for Someone Higher Up. Perhaps, too, I might be expelled from the country on the next plane. But that didn't seem reasonable.

The setup was there; it must be for some purpose that I could not yet understand.

"Where will the Señor be staying?" he said, after all the button-up was finished. He looked a little mussed, but not much the worse for wear. I told him the Hotel Parado.

I picked up my bags again and we went out. I followed the signs to the taxi stands — and was lucky enough to find one. Most of the other passengers were crowding into a bus.

A dark Cuban about thirty-five passed me. There was a sudden shock of recognition. Under his arm he was carrying a Spanish translation of Maugham's *The Moon and Sixpence*. This was the contact code-device that Brent had told me about. He paused at the curb and looked around. I went up to him.

I looked at the book. " 'Tis a good story," I said, nodding.

"He knows his men," said the Cuban in English, giving the rest of the recognition code. Then he opened the book, and appeared to be reading, but spoke softly out of the corner of his mouth.

"The customs agent is a pimp for old Pipon," he said. "You'll probably hear from him as soon as the film's developed."

That remark jolted me. How he had known was of course none of my business. I almost began to blush.

The guy went on murmuring. "You are free to wander around anywhere you want," he said. "Take pictures. Look like a tourist. Try to be as conspicuous as possible. And act dumb." A momentary smile played on his face, as if he had read an amusing sentence.

"Okay," I muttered.

After I got settled in the somewhat bleak room at the Hotel Parado, I took his advice. To say that I was a sensation in Havana would be the understatement of all time. Little kids followed me, hollering. Old men's eyebrows went up, and I heard their remarks about the kilt — always much the same: "Does he wear anything beneath?" was the general tenor of what they said. Young queens made eyes at me as I walked in the hot sunshine of the lazy tropical afternoons for the next two days. Young girls eyed me giggling, and whispered behind their hands.

Without much trouble I found all the cruisy spots of Havana. One of the main ones was the Manzana de Gomez, a building that took up a whole block, but was built around a central court with a plaza. The department stores were especially interesting, filled with boys I would have liked to have a flop with. And the Calle St. Obispo, which ran from the Manzana to Habana Street in the old section, was lined with young men lounging on the sidewalk cruising. It looked as if Uncle Fidel's edict had not enjoyed much enforcement.

True to the tourist ideal, I did everything that was expected of me. I visited the Capitolia where the "lawmakers" hung out and did their business, and noticed that the great diamond was still there, set in the floor of the rotunda and well-guarded. I asked about it even though I knew that it was the centerpoint from which all distances in Cuba were measured, and wondered how soon it would find its way into Uncle Faithful's treasure house.

It was on the evening of the third day that a bellboy knocked at my door in the hotel, and handed me an envelope bearing my name. I thanked him, tipped him (although I knew he was not supposed to take it), and shut the door.

The envelope contained a heavy white card with the inscription printed in flowing letters: "The Minister of War, Camillo Fajardo, requests the presence of"—and here my name was written in—"at a reception at his house at 77, Avenida del Monte, on the evening of—" and there was a curious thing. "Friday, at eight p.m." was also written in by hand!

I sat on the edge of the bed looking at the thing, and wondering why the date and time should be inscribed rather than printed. Could it be that old Pipon had a whole stack of these, and simply used them when he found someone he wanted?

Then another thought struck me. Poor Marcel, the little steward from Air France! He'd be disappointed. But, I thought as I shrugged, he could go down to the Malecón by the waterfront and take his pick from all the kids sitting on the wall.

Maybe I'd see him on the way back. But you had to put first things first.

Dusk had fallen on that Friday evening—a warm purple Cuban dusk, lazy and tropical, with a fugitive breeze stirring the leaves on the trees. I walked down the Prado, the main drag, towards my rendezvous with old Pipon on the Avenida del Monte. The Prado was an attractive boulevard with benches on both sides and a little parkway down the middle. And the benches were full of attractive laughing young men, their white shirts open to the navel, their brown chests gleaming under the occasional light of the moon, now and then shadowed by a few black and silver clouds.

It was hard to think of Pipon with all that stuff around me. Sex breathed from the sidewalks, and the air was full of a hot sensuality. My kilt and costume brought out a series of wolf-whistles and obscene remarks in Spanish, all of which I understood, and some of which were very funny. And then I turned on to the Avenida del Monte, leaving it all behind.

A shadow detached itself from a dark patch under a tree. I saw the familiar book that my contact carried.

"Jock," he said. "Watch out for his old trick. He'll put a knock-out pill in the brandy after dinner. Pour it out if you can. You'll be eating on the terrace, and there's a potted palm close to the chaise longue."

"You've got all this down pretty well," I said.

"Yeah," the guy said. If he were really Cuban, he'd certainly been educated in the States. "Your bags are already on the way to the airport. A soon as you can, head straight for there. We'll have a car waiting out front, and the gate won't be locked—by the time we get through with it. There may be some violence. He's got a gun on him all the time. Be careful . . ."

It was all in a whisper, hardly louder than the night air . . . He went on. "You'll take the midnight plane to Paris. Your ticket's at the Air France counter. Just ask for it."

He stuck out his hand. I shook it, and he held it a little longer than a spy should. "Hope we meet again sometime," he whispered, and I saw his white teeth gleam. "I'd kinda like to see for myself what's under that kilt."

"Anytime, Mac," I said.

He faded back into the shadows, and I went on. My heart was beating heavily and my armpits were wet. I took a few deep breaths to get control of myself, and managed. But the sense of danger remained, flooding me with adrenalin and excitement . . .

Number 22 was surrounded by a high wall with iron spikes on top, and guarded by an iron gate. There was no sentry there, however. I pushed at the latch and it opened. Then I walked up a winding driveway, through the warm air heady with the scent of frangipani and gardenia. The gentle nightwind blew free under my kilt. It felt so good that I found myself wishing that I could wear one all the time.

But it was absolutely quiet—no cars, no people, as you might expect at a big reception. I was more sure than ever there would be no one else. The front rooms blazed with light, and the old mansion with its white columns could have come straight out of the antebellum South in the United States.

I pulled at the old-fashioned bell-handle, and heard the ring of chimes far in the house. And waited.

The door opened at last. A handsome black-haired white-coated young man stood there.

"I have this," I said to him in English, extending the white card of my invitation. He smiled a little and did not even look at it.

"Señor Fajardo is expecting you," he said. Curious how the sibilant 's,' pronounced by a gay one, is recognizable in any language.

He stood aside to let me enter.

A crystal chandelier, a parquet floor gleaming like topaz, and baroque frills everywhere. It was all white and golden, like the entry hall to an eighteenth-century French château. A staircase with red carpet spiraled up to a balcony that swept in a circle around the entire room.

"The Señor will please follow me?" the young servant said. His buttocks were tight and hard under the black trousers, so fitted the crease in his ass showed. Our heels echoed on the golden wooden floor.

He led me through another room—this one heavily carpeted, with an ornate rosewood grand piano, bookshelves filled with leather bindings, and tables bearing candelabra. It was like a Hollywood conception of aristocratic elegance. Damn, I thought—if this is the way the representatives of the Peoples' Government of Cuba live, it might be nice to change over.

The young man paused at one of the tall glass doors, and opened it full on the terrace and the sweet Cuban night. He said, in Spanish, "The Señor from Scotland is here," and stood aside for me.

A gross and grotesque figure arose from a chaise longue. "Welcome," he said in a heavy English, advancing towards me and extending a great fat paw. "I am Camillo Fajardo." He grinned widely.

97

Pipon lived up to his nickname—Potbelly. His heavy pendulous stomach sagged down over the belt of his fatigue uniform, the standard dress of all the regime. Like the Leader, his beard was big, bushy, and black. His hairline was receding, and what was left of his hair hung thick and oily like a beatnik's down to his shoulders.

I shook his hand, which was hot and clammy-wet, and tried not to notice the three rings on it. He wore an overpowering heavy-sweet perfume which swept over me in waves. "I am Jock McAndrews." And then I looked around, pretending to be puzzled. "I thought there was to be a reception . . . that is . . ."

Pipon shrugged expansively. "Is it not so?" he said, smiling with bad teeth. "I, Camillo Fajardo, receive the visitor from Scotland, and offer him the hospitality of our house and country. Will you be seated?"

I pulled the kilt around forwards, bunching it above the center of my crotch as I had learned to do, and sat down. Then he addressed the young man in Spanish. "Emilio, leave the amontillado, and see that all is in readiness. After we eat, bring the brandy, and then you may go for the evening."

He turned back to me. "I am honored that you should grace this house," he said, and attempted a small bow, but his belly hardly permitted him to carry through with it.

For a moment I had an odd regret. I was here to betray him, yes—for the "good of my country"—whatever that was. But there was something more. He was one like me . . . and does not the bond of the homosexual override all distinctions, of class, wealth, and status—and perhaps even patriotism? But then my common sense took over, and the practical asserted itself. I was committed. And of all the brands that man can wear, I found 'traitor' more obnoxious than 'queer.' The momentary pity fled into the night, and reality returned. Besides . . . what would the American troops do to me when they eventually tramped the streets of Havana, sometime in the far future? The rim I lived on was narrow enough as it was.

The boy returned with tall thin sherry glasses on a tray, and I took one. It was the very best sherry, sweet and nutlike. The terrace floor gleamed blackly, and the white marble railing sliced through the warm darkness. Beyond it I glimpsed a formal garden, blooming with shadowed flowers. It was a night for hedonists like me.

Pipon was talking—sometimes slowly, searching for words. The man was really intelligent, and he knew what was going on in the world outside the little fortress of Cuba. He spoke of Paris, the ballet, the theatre—and then finally the movies.

"Have you ever appeared in the cinema, Señor?" he asked slyly. His question brought me back with a sudden thump to my task.

"Na," I said, " 'tis na bra' and handsome enough I be. Ye jest with me."

And then, behind a delicately filigreed screen nearby, I saw what could only be the outline of a small movie screen on a standard, and a darker shadow that was perhaps the projector. I began to sweat a little. My performance at customs . . .? I'd have to get that damned reel out before I left . . .

The supper was as elegant as the surroundings—cold pheasant, chilled sauterne from France, a salad, a mold of chickpeas and tiny green beans in a highly-sauced good old American gelatin. And more wine. He handled the silver deftly, talking all the while. And then when we had finished, he rang a small silver bell. Emilio appeared with two huge brandy snifters, big as Tartar heads, and a bottle of Napoleon.

"Thank you, Emilio," Pipon said again in Spanish. "You may leave now, but be back before dawn. Lock the gate as you leave."

Emilio smiled, bowed, and started back towards the house.

At that moment I decided that I might as well give old Pipon the chance to doctor my drink like a gentleman. I half-rose to my feet."Er . . ." I said, "all that wine . . . could I be excused for a moment?"

"But certainly," said Pipon, and called to Emilio. "Show the Señor from Scotland the way."

Emilio smiled at the door and waited for me. He led me through the carpeted room, and then up the great curved stairway. I watched the working of the muscles in his legs and buttocks as he preceded me. He was a lovely Latin lover-boy.

The bathroom was done in black and white marble, with a sunken tub and gold faucets. Emilio preceded me into the room, and then closed the door behind him. Swiftly, he fell to his knees and clasped me around the thighs with one arm, while with the free hand he started to lift my kilt.

"Just a moment, kid," I said, lapsing into American slang with

99

my surprise. "There's a little matter first . . ."

Emilio shook his head violently. "No . . . here . . ." he said, and opened his mouth.

Well, there's no accounting for tastes, as the old lady said when she kissed the cow. I helped Emilio on his way to happiness.

But then he seized on me and started to work in earnest. I began to pull away. "Later, me bra' laddie," I said. "Later. 'Tis na' wise to be so long gone."

It was like trying to disengage an octopus or a leech, but I succeeded. Then I rearranged my kilt a little and opened the door. The last I saw of him, he was still kneeling disconsolately on the marble floor, with—as the French have it—"the door of the grocery open and all the vegetables in view." The merchandise looked extraordinarily fine, and I regretted not being able to stay to partake of it.

I came back from the bathroom warmed from the wine and the encounter with Emilio but still in control of myself. Pipon was sitting in a chair, leaning back against the cushions, with the two round snifters of brandy beside him. I supposed that by then the pill had been safely dissolved in one of them.

He motioned me to the chaise longue and I sat down, leaning against the cushions. The position I took put me as close as possible to the sheltering palm that grew from its pot behind the chaise longue.

Smiling, Pipon raised his huge bulk from the metal chair and brought me one of the huge glasses. I cupped my hand underneath it, the stem between my fingers; it fitted my palm like the huge cold breast of a female corpse.

"Ye are a perfect host," I said, swirling the brandy and smiling up at him.

"To our friendship," he said, and raised his glass.

I was caught. I smiled a little crookedly, and put the glass to my mouth. Then with closed lips I pretended to drink, and made my throat seem to swallow. I took the glass away and smiled again.

" 'Tis right tasty," I said, swirling the glass still so that he could not see if I had taken any. I put my nose to the open end of it and breathed deeply. The sharp aromatic smell of the brandy rose in my nostrils. Then I uncrossed my legs and with my body slid down a little, so that my kilt hitched higher. The potted palm was two feet away from me; I had to distract him.

100

From the angle where he was sitting, I am sure that the movement with my kilt succeeded, and that he had caught a glimpse of what lay long and heavy beneath it. Suddenly his hand trembled. He set his own glass on the table and reached into his pocket, pulling out a handkerchief. But I must really have shaken him because he fumbled with it, and dropped it on the floor.

He bent over for it, and I reached to dump the brandy into the palm pot. Then I quickly brought the glass back to my lips and pretended to be draining it by the time he recovered the handkerchief over the great rotundity of his belly.

"Och," I said, and smacked my lips. " 'Tis delicious."

Pipon wiped his perspiring face with the handkerchief.

I placed the glass carefully on the floor and lay back on the chaise longue again, my hands behind my head, and my legs spread as wide as the chaise would permit. This time I knew very well that I was exposed. I could feel the warm air blowing on my crotch. My kilt was more than halfway up my thighs. I yawned mightily.

"So-o-o warm," I said sleepily, and yawned again. "So . . . much good food . . . and wine." I closed my eyes.

Come now or never, I thought. I heard him pick up his own glass, drink noisily, and then set it down again. The chair creaked a little as he raised his great weight from it. Then I let my head fall sidewise, and my body relax completely. I also let one arm slip down, so that my knuckles touched the cool floor. I sensed him kneeling by the chaise longue. The rough fabric of his uniform brushed against my fingertips, and I felt his trembling fingers lift the kilt higher, and higher. He turned the kilt and sporran back and laid it gently on my chest, so that I was completely naked where it counted most.

And then—then! Goddlemighty! I had forgotten about his beard! It was a good eight inches long and bushy, and with the first contact it made between my legs I needed every ounce of control and tension that I possessed to keep from jumping straight towards the sky, roaring with laughter. It tickled—god, how it tickled! I wanted to laugh, to giggle, to scream. I felt the skin in goose bumps all over my neck and shoulders and legs as he bore down with that device of the devil. It was like feathers and metal scouring-pads combined, and then in the midst of the wire there suddenly appeared a hot moist clamp that fitted over me and drew me down, down and inwards, with great talent.

Gradually the fatal desire to laugh, to twitch, began to leave. Now the wire predominated, and I felt the tender skin between my legs was being rubbed raw and hot. Gahdamn, I thought — the things I've done for my country. But then another sensation came, too. I began to grow excited — after all, a man can endure just so much, and self-control has its limits.

But I was not certain whether whatever drug he had given me would have allowed me to turn ramrod. I supposed it would not hinder the natural course of events — else what pleasure in it all for him? I wondered if I could permit myself a small moan . . .

And then, even with my eyelids closed, I saw the white hell break — in the general direction of the white-columned railing. In three seconds the team of photographers must have popped twelve or fourteen flashbulbs. They had evidently been hiding in the garden. Blinded, as I opened my eyes, I quickly looked away; but my eyes retained a red circle of light, turning slowly green, floating wherever I tried to focus.

I heard Pipon roar with anger and saw him fumbling at his belt for his gun. He had evidently been blinded too.

This was it. I looked in his direction, and saw the green circle floating where his head should have been. It made it a little easier, not to have to look him in the face. With all my strength I landed a sidewise karate blow, directly through the beard at his Adam's apple.

He fell over like an ox, clutching his shattered windpipe, and retching. I sprang to my feet, still excited, with the sporran sticking straight out in front of me. I was able to see a little better now.

The photographers had vanished. All was still, save for the noises that old Pipon was making as he writhed on the floor. A little vomit crept out of his lips.

I leaped for the filigreed screen and wrenched at the projector, pulling the film off the spindle and fumbling to get the already threaded part as well. Then I dashed for the front door, running like a maniac, kilt flying, heart pounding, and hearing all the legions of Cuba after me in hot pursuit.

But the gate was open — broken, really — and the car was waiting. And there was no trouble at the airport.

And even one small thing to comfort me. Marcel was the steward on the way back. And he finished what Emilio and old Pipon had begun—and then finished it again. And again.

That was it—except for a few details.

A week later I lay naked in the morning on a bed in the Hôtel Crillon in Paris, overlooking the sunny Place de la Concorde. My suite was one of the most expensive in the most expensive hotel in all Paris, but it cost me nothing. I had just finished reading in *Le Figaro* about the great administrative shakeup in Cuba, and how Camillo Fajardo had suffered a nervous breakdown arising from a throat ailment, and been sent away to a clinic for his health.

A cablegram had arrived that morning, too. It was crumpled on the floor, staring up at me. In a way it was the most satisfying detail of the whole adventure. It said simply: "Will you work for us further at double former salary question Brent."

I had already answered it with a one-word message: "No."

And then I rose lazily from the bed and went to the windows, feeling the silken texture of the rug against my bare feet. I reached out and closed the shutters of the windows against the sunny morning, and pulled the drapes to create a violet gloom around me. Then I hauled out the rented screen and projector, set it running, and for about the tenth time that week, lay back on the bed to watch a really good four hundred feet of film, starring a handsome Scot whom I used to know pretty well, once upon a time.

The Pool Cue

"Well, here I am again," said the young voice over the telephone.

Deep within I groaned silently to myself, and looked out at the San Francisco afternoon, grey for a change. And then I summoned up a bright inflection, and said, "What brings you back to Sodom and Gomorrah?"

"I'm working for a guy who runs a puppet show," Clint said, "and I drove out with him from Chicago."

"Where are you staying?"

"At the Hilton," he said proudly. "And the show's at the Fairmont. Then we have another one in Oakland."

"Looks like you're coming up in the world," I said. At least, if he were with someone else, I wouldn't be bothered with him and his sad little adolescent jokes. "Well, come see me some time," I added, thinking that the coffee ought to come off the stove.

But he was not to be turned aside so easily. "I heard my brother came out here last time lookin' for me."

"Yeah," I said, "and I made him."

Clint giggled. "Like you always said you wanted."

"Sure," I said. "At least he's one member of your family who doesn't lie flat on his back like a sack of potatoes. Like you and your two other triplet brothers."

"Maybe I've changed," he said.

"I doubt it." I saw that the conversation could go on for the whole afternoon. "Listen, Clint," I said. "I've got to take the coffee off the stove. Call me up some other time, huh?"

104

"Sure," he said, and we hung up.

The truth is that we all change from time to time, and as we grow more jaded in this crazy hummingbird life of ours, we go on to newer novelties. What they are is unpredictable. We may turn to the S/M game, or to foot fetishism, or to exotic types such as Polynesians, Eskimos, Asians, or cops. I'd been through a good deal since Clint left San Francisco the last time—and had settled on one thing at the moment which brought me a good deal of satisfaction: blacks, the image of God cut in ebony, and the blacker the better.

It was hard to say what I liked about them so much, whether their joyous abandon in bed, their lack of remorse or a sense of shame after it was all over, their smashed African faces, their abilities at lovemaking, their reputed size of what mattered, their wide shoulders and narrow hips and long legs, the harsh male smell of them, the feel of their hard black-curled hair—when it was not straightened, or 'gassed' as they phrased it. But at any rate in my Black Period, the thought of motionless Clint, white as milk, lanky and nonmuscled, unable to react no matter how long one worked, left me about as excited as the prospect of feasting on strawberries smothered in lard.

And the blacks were numerous and available in San Francisco, or that failing, Oakland and Berkeley, where the whiteys were actually outnumbered. But in the city, the Magic City as we who lived in San Francisco called it, there was a club on Eddy Street called the Bettermen—why, no one knew except that it was a close take-off on the name of a general who had done big things for San Francisco. It was legally a private club, with dancing afterhours, and beer drinking, and a couple of pool tables in the back room. And it was a source of supply, one might say, for here both black and white hustlers, habitués of the Tenderloin district in the city, met to let off steam . . . and find their bed partners.

So, with such a source—what need had I to concern myself with Clint?

But I might have known I couldn't win. The puppeteer went back to Chicago, leaving Clint in San Francisco, and early one morning there came a ring at the door. Full of sleep I went to answer it—and there he stood, grinning his crooked grin (his teeth were much worse), carrying a suitcase and a smaller zippered leather case that looked as if it might be a container for a precious violin bow.

"What the hell," I said.

"Can I come in?" he said, putting on as much charm as he could, which was not much as far as I was concerned.

I opened the door without saying anything and he came in. "Can I stay with you for a few days?" he asked. "I'm gonna get a job out here."

"Seems to me I've heard that one before," I said grumpily.

"No, honest," he said. "This time I really am. I've already applied at three service stations."

"Humph," I said.

"I got some money," he said. "Enough to hold me until I get my first paycheck."

"*If* you get a job," I said sourly.

"I will," he said confidently.

"All right," I said. "But there are certain house rules. You set up your folding bed every night, and you fold it up again in the morning. And you buy your own food. And then as soon as your second paycheck comes, you move out into a room of your own. Or an apartment. I need my privacy."

"You won't even know I'm here," he promised.

And so it began. Oddly enough, he did get a job at a gasoline station, only two days after he arrived. But I did know he was there, for he landed the nightshift and that meant that I couldn't turn on my radio as I always did first thing in the morning when I awakened. It meant, too, that I had to pussyfoot around and not rattle the breakfast dishes, although from the way he slept—the profound quiet sleep of the young—I doubted that a flourish of trumpets in his ear would have brought him around.

He got his first paycheck. "Now you can leave," I said.

He looked down, somewhat ashamed. "You said the *second* one," he said. "I had to use most of this one to buy my uniforms for the station and to pay for laundering them. And I had to buy a pair of boots, 'cause all that grease was ruinin' my good shoes."

That much was true. The 'boots' were really calf-high paratrooper's shoes, with lots of lacing. I couldn't take my eyes off them. And Clint knew my weakness.

"Pretty, ain't they?" he said, holding one up by its top. I took it

106

from him, and almost involuntarily smelled the good fresh leather smell of it. "Yeah," I said, handing it back. But a small part of my icy shell melted in that moment and he seemed to know it. For he invented a little game: when he would come from work in the morning, I would hear him open and close the door softly. And then after a moment to take off his shoes—while I pretended to be asleep—he would come into the bedroom and with one swift gesture enclose my whole face in the open end of the boot, laughing as he did so.

"Pretty good way to wake up in the morning, huh?" he said. It was hard to be angry with him after that.

During those first two or three weeks we tried a little roll in the hay as we used to, but not much ever came of it. His immobility made me think too much of making love to a corpse, and finally we gave it up entirely. I was reminded of the old wives' tale that twins shared the same soul, and that each twin had therefore only half a soul. In the case of triplets, did each possess only one-third of a soul? And was the sexual urge divided equally as the soul was?

I think that Clint was a superb example of the truth of such folklore. His barely perceptible movements in bed were precisely one third of what they should have been. For a twenty-two-year-old, he was the most asexual man—with a man—I had ever known.

The curious long leather case with the zipper contained Clint's most prized possession: a professional cue stick that unscrewed in the middle. It was, he told me, a sixty-dollar cue—and I could believe him, for it was polished and gleaming, with brass fittings— phallic, straight, and strong. He played a lot of pool, and from what he said he was pretty good at it. "The balls just seem to know where to go when I hit 'em," he bragged. Judging from the money he earned from side bets, he must have been right.

From an active dislike of his presence, I gradually grew used to having him there when I got home from work. We are all lonely and we all ought to be married, either to a man or a woman or a dog.

October slipped into November, and that into December. The morning ritual of the shoe kept on. I found also that I did not need to keep quiet; even the alarm clock at his ear did not waken him.

But there was something wrong with me. I did not feel actually a part of the scene in the most glamorous and romantic city of the States. I had lived too long in Chicago; my taproots had been sunk there too deeply. There was only one cure for it.

"I think I'll have to go back to Chicago to kill it off," I said to him one day. "And I'll pick the worst season of the year there — over Christmas."

Clint looked out at the bright sunshine of the December morning, at the camellias growing beside the door and the goldfish swimming lazily in the pond among the white water lilies. "And leave all this for the snow and wind?"

"Yeah," I said. "And I'll make appointments with the dentist and the doctor, and have an eye examination — all at nine in the morning."

"How'll you ever make it?" he asked. "You can hardly get up at ten-thirty."

"That's the point," I said. "I want to kill off that nagging little feeling I have for the city. Zero weather, high winds, snow and slush — and having to get up early should do it."

"What do you want me to do?" he said. "Move out?"

I crossed my legs and pushed myself back in the chair. "Well," I said, "I guess I'll leave you here. You've talked so much about your honesty, and how you 'weren't brought up that way' — to steal anything, that is — that I guess I can trust you."

"Yeah, you can," he said.

"You're the only one I'd ever leave in the house alone," I said. "Thanks."

"Only one condition," I said. "Don't bring any of your female friends here."

He looked pained. "Of course not," he said.

And so I went to Chicago, and it was all as bad as I thought it would be. I could not understand what had ever made me love that city. The snow fell to a depth of eleven inches, the wind howled, the temperature slipped to zero; and through it all I was wading, puffing, and blowing to my early morning appointments. I forced myself to stay ten days, and then one night I called Clint.

"I'm coming back tomorrow," I said. "Everything all right?"

"Sure," he said. "How's the weather there?"

"Just what I expected," I said bitterly. "I'm tired of fighting it."

He laughed. "It's nice and warm here," he said. And then, "Oh, by the way, I quit my job."

"Just a drifter," I said. "What was wrong this time?"

"The station owner made me work too hard, and didn't pay me enough."

I sighed. "Why is it that all you young ones want to start at the top?"

"The best place," he said, and laughed again.

And so the plane deposited me the next day at the San Francisco airport. The curious looks I got from the people there annoyed me, but you could hardly blame them. For I was bundled up in boots, overcoat, and gloves—and it was warm and sunny when I landed. I could hardly wait to get home to shed my winter wear.

When I opened the door, the house seemed curiously empty. You can somehow feel if no one is there. There were no signs of Clint's occupancy. And then I saw the note lying on my chair—scrawled in green pencil on the back of an envelope. It said in his nearly illiterate way: "I am ashamed of myself so I go. I have taken your money from the bedroom and used it. This is what I am ashamed about I will some how send you yor money and hope we can still be friens at a latter date all thoug I wont blame you for not trustin me. With regretts I sign, Clint."

I had to sit down. The shock was intense. And almost unseeing, hardly knowing what I was doing, I took off my winter clothes and went to the bedroom. In a place that I had thought well-concealed and secret, I usually kept an 'operating' fund of about a hundred dollars. On top of the money, before I had gone, I had left a note saying: "This money is counted, Clint, so be governed accordingly." Evidently, deep under the iceberg of my subconscious I did not trust him at all, and never had.

He had found it, all right. The money was gone, the cupboard bare. I checked everything else as quickly as I could, and all seemed to be as I had left it. His clothes were not there, nor the boots, but nothing else of mine was missing. Like a true professional, he took only what could not be traced.

I was sick. It was not so much the theft of the money I resented as the utter destruction of my faith in Clint, and from then on in possibly every human being.

As I left the bedroom, I stepped on something that crunched. It was a bobby pin—and looking farther on the bedroom rug, I

109

found three more. I looked at my bed, unmade; he had been sleeping there. And then—shuddering—I went to get clean sheets and change the linens. As I folded up the dirty ones and reached behind the door to put them in the laundry bag, I saw the long black leather case of his pool cue standing in the corner.

The gush of hatred that swept over me left me weak and shaking. I picked up the damned thing and looked around. For a moment—like a bad-tempered child—I thought of breaking it, or burning it, or destroying it in some way. He had evidently forgotten it; certainly he would never have left it as a partial payment for the money he had stolen. I hefted it in my hand, and then threw it forcibly behind the door and closed it. But like some mysterious nuclear-powered device, it still sent out its waves of radiation.

It was dark outside by now. I looked at the lights winking down the hillside towards the center of town. And then—my curious rage still swollen in my throat and temples—I showered and shaved and put on my hustler's uniform, levis and boots and leather jacket, and headed for the central part of the city, towards the Bettermen Club.

As I drove to the center of town, I found that my rage was still with me, and like any ordinary bitch I laid plans to put out the word about Clint. I had several addresses in Chicago of his former 'clients'—so off would go notes to them, telling of the whole affair. And there were also notes to be sent to Los Angeles, New York, Tampa, Dallas, and elsewhere. As for San Francisco, I would take care of that myself. Word of a hustler's treachery has a way of coursing like lightning on the underground grapevine. I presumed that he had not yet gone far, and that he had probably lost himself in the raunchy Tenderloin district.

The Bettermen Club was as dingy as ever, especially the ceiling with its holes in the plaster, though hardly anyone ever looked upwards. Most club members were too eager to get in to see what other mammals or animals of prey were whooping it up around the corner of the L-shaped desk. It was early yet; there were not many there. The live combo did not start playing until two a.m.; before that, there was the jukebox to furnish music for dancing. Only a few couples were on the floor.

I wandered on through, back to the far room where there were

110

little talk-tables, and where the beer was sold, and the pool tables were. Again, there were not many in the back room either, for it was not yet the hour when the walkers of the streets started to come in. But both pool tables were busy, and I walked over to watch.

Then I saw him. He was possibly one of the best-looking blacks I had ever laid an eye on, tall and handsome like an African prince, and so black that when he stood in the shadows he almost disappeared from view. He should have been wearing a turban with jewels around his neck. He was playing the game with a nondescript little white faggot with shoulder-length blond hair who couldn't shoot worth a damn. I felt my heart begin to thud, felt the old familiar tug, and knew that I was going to get that blackamoor, sooner or later.

It was fascinating to watch him. Evidently the game had just started, for he still had on his suit-coat—a suit of iridescent green and blue that changed color under the lights like a beetle's wings, the kind of suit that black dandies love so much. He was a man in every sense—his laughter was male, his shoulders were broad, his legs long. There was none of the faggot's affectation about him. He wore his hair short, curled tight against his well-shaped head. His ears were tiny shells of jet, and his face had a pure African cast—lips full and dark. His chin was strong, with a small cleft in it. His movements around the table were lithe and panther-like, and his long fingers scampered like black butterflies over the green baize cloth of the table.

Mentally I undressed him, and clothed him as he should be— naked except for a glittering gold breechclout above his magnificent midnight thighs, his biceps encircled by broad golden bands. I discarded the idea of a turban and replaced it with a low crown of egret feathers, and set him on a golden throne, his legs spread wide, and his fourteen-inch-long feet carelessly placed on the steps below him.

I exhaled, and muttered "Sheez" under my breath. There was a transsexual called Sandy standing beside me—a tall thin boy who never wore anything but girl's clothes, and who was taking hormone shots in preparation for the time when he would have enough money for the 'Operation' that would technically change him into a woman.

111

Sandy heard me. "Sheez what?" she said lightly.

"Who's the stud in the blue-green suit?" I said.

"That's Jimmy," she said. "I don't know his last name."

"He sure plays a fancy game of pool."

"He's the best around here," Sandy said. "He's straight—or says he is."

"You been with him?"

Sandy made a little moue. "I'm married," she said. "But I wouldn't mind."

"He certainly has that mysterious factor of the real male," I said.

"You want to meet him?" Sandy said. "When he finishes the game, I'll introduce you."

Of course Jimmy won. The pale white faggot stamped his foot, tossed his blondined hair, and twitched his fat little ass over to the coke machine.

Sandy called Jimmy over to the table against which I was lounging, and introduced us. His handshake was firm, his hand moist from the exercise of the game.

"I'll leave you two lovebirds alone," Sandy said, with just the faintest trace of a smirk.

"Thanks, Sandy," I said. "I'll dance at your operation."

"Man," said Jimmy, looking after her. "I just don't understand."

I shrugged. "No need to bother," I said, and then changed the subject. "You're a wizard with that game," I said, nodding towards the table. "Best I ever saw."

"Thanks," he said briefly.

"You handle that cue like a professional," I said. "You play much?"

He laughed again. "Man, I'm a hustler," he said. "A pool hustler, that is."

"You straight?"

"Yep."

"Even for twenty bucks?"

He smiled. "I just don't go that route," he said. "Too much pussy around." But then he seemed to reconsider. He moved a little closer to me, where my hand was resting on the edge of the table, and pressed his crotch directly against the knuckles. "But you can feel it," he grinned. "Just to see what you're missing."

I was missing a lot. Then an idea struck me. "You got a cue-stick

112

of your own?" I said.

"No, man. Can't afford one."

"Well, I'll tell you something. Somebody left a sixty-dollar stick at my house. Leather case and all. And I don't want it around. I'd like to give it to someone, but it's too bad you're straight."

He put out both hands and clutched me hard on my upper arms. "You kiddin', man?" he said. He shook me a little.

"Not at all."

His eyes glittered in the shadows. "It in good condition?"

"Might need a coat of varnish, that's all," I said. "But then you're straight," I said ironically. "I better give it to a club member."

He tightened his grip. "Listen," he said. "I've wanted one for a long time. You mean you'll give it to me if we go to bed together?"

I nodded.

"How many times?"

"Just one for the bargain," I said. "But I can always hope, can't I?"

He laughed, his teeth dazzling to my eyes. "What's holdin' us?" he said. "You got wheels?"

"Of a sort," I said. "A Volkswagen."

"You live far?"

"Out by Golden Gate Park," I said.

He let go of one of my arms and kept his grip on the other, steering me out past the dancing couples, and the front desk. Eddie, who ran the place, looked up.

"That's the shortest visit you've paid us in quite a while," he said, leering.

I nodded as Jimmy hustled me towards the door. "It's just that you gotta know how," I said over my shoulder.

Eddie beckoned to me. I disengaged myself from Jimmy's grip, and bent my ear to hear what Eddie wanted to say. "You're the only one that ever made it outa here with him," he whispered. "What's the secret?"

I smiled. "Oh," I said. "It's an old voodoo trick I learned in Haiti. I'll show you how some time."

And then Jimmy and I went out into noise and drunkenness and the nice fresh gasoline fumes of the Tenderloin.

Perhaps, I thought, I had been a little hasty in condemning

Clint. In very few cases have I ever got so much for a mere sixty dollars, especially when you divide it by nearly twenty weeks. All my friends in the San Francisco area think it odd that I always am otherwise engaged when they ask me to come to visit them on Sunday evenings.

But they find it even more odd that I—never a sportsman in any way—should suddenly become so interested in the game of pool.

Jimmy's been teaching me, always on Sunday. I've never known anyone who could handle a pool cue the way he does his.

Anatomy of a Fiasco

The anger that I felt over the evening's fiasco hadn't left me by the time I got home to my hideaway in Berkeley. It's stupid to kick furniture or doors, but I delivered a smash to my gate as I came in that rattled the fencepost and started the neighbor's dogs barking.

But it was all my own fault. I'd had a trick at the Hilton Hotel in San Francisco, and everything seemed to be going fine. He was somewhat older—white-haired and very distinguished looking, and he had a large and elegant suite up in the tower. We had met on the street—a glance, a cupping of my crotch (not seeming intentional, but rather an absent-minded adjustment), a few words exchanged, a room number given as we momentarily parted—and I sailed right through the lobby, my leather jacket and levis no more noticeable than the crummy-looking tourists who were flocking around the registration desk.

"Would you like a drink?" he asked in a cultured but not effeminate voice.

"Sure," I said.

"You look like a bourbon man," he said.

"Right you are," I said, and then thought that perhaps he would think I was mimicking his faintly British accent, so I added: "Dat's okay—just a little water." I didn't even say "branch water."

He went to make it. I saw a copy of Firbank's collected works on the night stand. "Sheez," I said. "I haven't read *Cardinal Pirelli* for a helluva long time."

A strange look came over his face. He very carefully set down the bourbon on the table beside the book.

"You know Firbank's writing?" he said, halfway strangling on the last word.

"Yeah."

I guess a dramatist would call it a pregnant pause.

"I'm sorry," he said. "You've spoiled the image. I had hoped . . ."

I saw what had happened. "No—I'm the one who's sorry," I said, seeing the fifty bucks go sailing out the window.

He looked down at the carpet. "I suppose you understand."

"Right you are," I said, this time imitating his accent deliberately. "I'll know better next time."

So there it was. Blown sky-high. Teach you to show off, I thought. But it had all happened without my thinking it through. He wanted a rough stud, not a reader of Firbank. I'd made a mistake.

Greeks ought not to drink when they're angry, for they have a dim cellular memory of Achilles shot with an arrow in the heel, of thunderbolts and catapults, and of the axe Hephaestus used to split open the head of Zeus. But I wanted the shot of bourbon that I had been denied by Mademoiselle Firbank. So on the way home I stopped off at a dingy little neighborhood bar called W&S—which over the years had been called Whip & Saddle, Wimps & Sissies, and Walk-in & Stagger-out—and many other things.

The lighting was low and there were only two persons there, with the gap-toothed bartender polishing a glass. One was fat and fifty and sat near the door. The other . . . *damn!*

He was about my height—six-one or two, and he sat straight-spined on the bar stool, one ankle crossed over his knee—boots and levis like my own—the real thing, no designer job—a T-shirt, and a clear cold look in his eyes that made the big vein in my throat start to chug.

Obviously, he was Italian. His hair was black—or was that a glint of copper, or a fluke from the pink light over his head? The thighs looked as if they had been sculptured by Praxiteles; the chest capable of the flight of Daedalus. I looked for wings—there were none. The face was clean-shaven and classic—the nose bearing straight down from the forehead, the eyebrows black and nearly joined at the center. His cheekbones were high and there was a faint blue shadow beneath them, whether from the beard-

116

mark or the hollows of that superb skull formation I could not tell.

There was a slight quirk to his mouth as he turned to look in my direction—a part smile.

I plunked myself down on the stool right next to him. "How's it goin'?" I asked.

He grinned. "Okay," he said. "What're you so mad about?"

"Does it show that much?" I growled.

"Sure does."

"Ah . . . a trick stood me up."

An eyebrow took flight, the right one, I guess. "You hustlin'?" he asked.

"Yep."

"So'm I." He stuck out his big hand and I shook it. "My name's Prospero," he said.

Oh lord, I thought, not twice in one night! I swallowed some bourbon and said casually, "I think I've heard that name before somewhere."

"Yes," he said. "It's from an old play somebody wrote once. Called 'A Summer Dream' or sumpin' like that."

I exhaled slowly, thinking of tempests and sea change. No danger of rejection for literature here. "Yeah," I said, "I guess I heard of it too, way back in high school."

"Most people call me Pross nowadays," he said, grinning. "But I ain't so fuckin' prosperous."

I waggled my hand. "Comes and goes," I said. "I'm Phil Andros."

For some reason we shook hands again, and my skin tingled. The magnetism that came out of him was almost overpowering. I knew one thing: I wanted to go to bed with Prospero. A vibrant attraction breathed out from him; it struck me and enfolded me like a golden laurentian spray. I looked at his face, his magnificent arms, his narrow waist—and I thought, sheez, he'd make a fine top man—just for a change. I wondered about what was going on in the dark valleys of my brain—whether I had too many x chromosomes or just not enough of the y ones, but something was happening which made ole Betsy stir in her warm tight nest and unfold a little. I reached down to adjust the swelling between my legs.

He saw the gesture and smiled.

"You doin' anything tonight?" I asked.

He looked at his glass, twirled it, and said, "Yeah, I'm waitin' for a john."

"Oh," I said, diminished.

"But listen," he went on. "How's about tomorrow? 'Bout this same time."

"Okay," I said. "I live just a coupla blocks away."

We exchanged telephone numbers and I gave him my address.

"See you here tomorrow night," he said.

I left then, heart pounding, breath short, and sweating more than the night demanded. But it sure as hell didn't keep me from giving the gate a double kick when I let it slam behind me as I came home. Nor from enfolding myself, in bed later, to visit Old Mrs. Palm and her five daughters. With a companion. Never ask me who.

We met in the same shabby bar the next evening, neither of us standing the other up, and had a coupla beers. Then we walked the few blocks to my house. It would have been interesting to have been followed by a movie camera, to record which of us had more success in out-swaggering the other. The butch talk was amusing too—and we each bragged about the number of our conquests, both male and female, although Pross seemed to favor the women. He'd had one marriage and one shack-up, leaving a kid in each place. I beat him out by claiming I'd had three—and god knew how many little bastards were running around Ohio and Illinois. To tell the truth, if there had been even one I would have counted it a miracle of the first order.

"What do you like to do in bed?" I asked, after we had shut the front door.

He made a flat motion with his hand. "Anything," he said. "But you know us wops. I'm gonna screw you."

"No way," I said, making the same gesture.

"Either I puts it up yours or you don't get me," he said, frowning a little.

"We'll think about it," I said. You arrogant son-of-a-bitch, I thought. But I didn't say it for at that moment he took off his T-shirt, and his torso stopped any complaint I had in mind.

His skin was that of a "white" Mediterranean, soft and smooth and almost luminous, insted of the dark swarthiness that Italians often have. It almost glowed. Each nipple shone like a small garnet on an areola of deep brown. Instead of the shapeless rolls of flesh

118

above the hips, the love handles, he had only the beginning of the strong ligament that swoops down the groin. It was cut off sharply by his belt, and then rose again on the other side, having—I knew—caressed his genitals in their hiding place. Above his left nipple, tattooed in a neat and curving arc, was the word "Prospero." My mouth moved in a curious way, almost as if I were about to taste some exotic fruit.

"Go douche," he said darkly.

"After I watch you undress," I said.

He almost smirked. "Oh ho!" he said.

"If the rest of you's as good as your top half," I said, poking my tongue into my cheek, "you may be a winner."

"It's better," he said, with a touch of smugness.

It was. He stood almost as if confined within a magic circle, while he began a slow-paced ritual all his own. Kneeling, he undid the straps of his boots, and then casually, looking with a conqueror's eye at me, pulled them off, first one and then the other. Then he slowly unbuckled his belt, standing, and with big strong fingers unbuttoned his fly—no foolish zipper there. Balanced on one leg, he drew the other out of his tight levis, peeling them down, and drawing his foot slowly through the opening.

He was without underwear, naturally. Show me a hustler who wears it and I'll show you someone not yet sure of himself.

I let out a low whistle. "Sheez," I said, looking at his thighs, darkened with his black body hair, and at the father of all evil, dangling, swinging, heavy with the engorging blood. The head of it in this light was almost purple. The columns of his thighs and calves were stupendous, and each muscle stood out in the sidelighting from the table lamp.

"Damn," I said with a dry mouth. "You look like Adonis. Or Apollo."

He looked at me. "I knew a guy named Apollo oncet," he said. "He was a little shrimp." Then he scowled. "Now, get after it, buddy. The bathroom."

Strangely enough, I didn't mind obeying him at all. When I finished my task I went back to the living room but he wasn't there. I looked in the bedroom. He had pulled down the cover and lay on the sheet, and turned on the dimmer for the overhead light. He had his arms behind his head. The black shadows of his armpit hair

119

and the triangle at his crotch gleamed dark-blue in the half-light.

He stretched like a black panther or some other great sensual cat. "You know what I'd like?" he asked, suddenly raising on one elbow.

I hardly knew what was going on inside me. From a macho hustler who rarely kissed, who had usually been nothing but trade, I suddenly felt the y chromosomes rattle against each other and go active. When I began "the life," I was sure I was straight, but a thousand beddings later I began to wonder. And a thousand after that—I began to look and lust and want things I had never wanted before. I'd fallen "in love" with guys a half-dozen times, and could name them all—but now it seemed that I was drunk with a character from Shakespeare, and wanted desperately to do everything that he told me, as long as he waved his magic wand.

"Well," he said again. "I asked you—do you know what I'd like first?"

I shook my head, not quite able to speak.

"A toe-job," he said, and stretched in that catlike way again, exhaling. "So, why don't you get with it, Mac?"

I did. Even his feet were beautiful—high-arched and long-toed, with the second toe classically long, longer than the big toe. I'd had many toe-jobs myself, but this was about only the second time I'd bent my head to the foot.

The skin was faintly moist from the wool sock he had been wearing, and the odor clean and fresh like new-turned earth. When I took the first toe in my mouth, the big one, it felt huge as a cock, and I used all the tricks I could remember that had ever been used on me, thinking even of Karl in the shoeshop in San Francisco.

I pointed my tongue, then made it loose and soft, and did a figure eight around each toe, licking and breathing the maleness of him—first one foot and then the other. He was moaning a little and turning his head from side to side on the pillow. One hand stretched down to his cock and cupped his balls, for his hardon was complete. Another drop of blood in it and it would have burst. From my position at his feet I reached up to take hold of it and felt it throb in my hand.

He sighed. "Buddy," he said, "you're okay. But now I gotta screw you. Get up from there and bend your ass over the edge of the bed here."

120

I did, wondering if he knew how to open the door. He laid a finger into my crack, and I felt the coolness of handcream from the jar that stood ever ready. Then I heard the soft *glistening* sound as he rubbed some more cream on his cock.

The first casual touch made me jump a little. He stroked the head of it up and then down the crack, poking gently here and there, higher then lower, but always returning to the celestial gate. I cast all doubt aside: he *did* know how to open doors!

And then slowly, inch by happy inch, I felt him enter. There was no pain at all. The path was open and prepared.

Possibly twice before in my life—once in Rome, once in Paris—I had had an experience so intense. I felt as if my whole being, soul and everything, had receded to my ass, and that someone was ascending the golden stairs to heaven, shaken with crystal, balmed with myrrh. Oddly, I remembered—a flash!—the young kilted Scot in Paris who spoke of his lover: "Ah, and when yer man is in ye, and he pulls ye on yer back on top of him, and ye're lookin' at the stars and smellin' of the heather, then ye know ye're in heaven!"

Well, there was no smell of heather around, but the stars I saw with tight-clenched eyelids, conjured out of the sheet against which my eyes were pressed, were real enough.

When he got going, he was the champion. With circular movements he touched every crevice and crypt. His hips swayed, his knees bent—and with deep thrusts alternating with small touchings and throbbings against the outer door, he teased and then comforted. Part of the time he seized me by the hipbones, and worked slowly and softly, like Ariel; at other moments his thrusts were cruel and deep, and I felt the rough hair against my ass as if Caliban were behind me. And then the tempo increased—his breathing grew hard and quick, and he burst within me, time after time, finally slowing, and chuckling a little.

And I had joined him in my own moment of dazzling stars, panting, and feeling myself slippery against the sheet of the bed. Prospero had more than a magic wand to tame the elements. He had tamed me.

Everyone has secrets—some large, some small—memories of failed performances, of things done when drunk (or sober), of foolishness committed in business, love, or daily living. Perhaps

121

you hide your baldness under a rug, or tell no one about the dental bridge. Perhaps like the French you may wear a "fascinator"—a long tube of carved sponge rubber pinned to the inside of your fly. Perhaps you have a testicle made of plastic, inserted where there was only an empty pocket. These secrets are yours, and yours alone.

The secret that I guarded from the world was the Thursday visit from Prospero. For six days a week I let the world look on me as the macho stud—confident, with body language indicating my availability—no feminine gestures or actions, no diffidence or uncertainty, the swagger carefully calculated, the look cool, appraising, and inviting. I was selling something, myself, my body, my prick—and enjoying it all the way. But on that one night a week, it was with dismay and yet a kind of real pleasure that I saw the facade waver and dissolve. Six days a top, one night a bottom—the proportion was disturbing, but I could stand it, for the sensations I received from my stud more than made up for the alarm I felt for myself.

It went on for many weeks. And then there came a special night when we both got stoned on sinsemilla, or perhaps it was Thai stick or some such. But that night—which began late, about midnight—went on until dawn. I don't remember it all—there was a lot of wrestling on the battleground of the bed, some giggling when I stuttered to him: "You be he-moth, I be she-moth" (although with a blank look he sobered enough to say, "Wot's a behemoth?"), a lot of entangling of bodies, lips here, there, and everywhere, and always the pulsing, demanding column of his flesh seeking and finding entry—one, two, three, a half-dozen times—until the window slowly grew a glimmering square. And then when the seventh time arrived, he failed utterly. No caressing of that cock succeeded, nothing could bring it to life.

"Gahdamn," he swore softly, his right hand ceasing its labors. "My arm's 'bout wore out. I guess it's over."

I watched the ceiling swim in a slow circle above my head. I was exhausted myself, and had a brand-new center of consciousness to remind me of our night of grass and roses.

"Yeah," I said. "You've worn me out too. Maybe it's time to get some sleep."

Suddenly he raised up on one elbow. "Not yet," he said. "Us

122

wops don't give up that easy."

His face was close to mine. We had never kissed, and yet at that moment I felt an overwhelming urge to do so. I made a tentative movement with my arm but he stopped me.

"Tell you what," he said, lying down again on his back and poking me roughly on the shoulder. "You get up and straddle me and stick it in my mouth. That always gives me a hardon."

For a moment I did not believe that I had heard him right. And then my brain played it again for my ear.

"*What?*" I said, harshly.

"You heard me," he said. "Just climb on top and stick it in my mouth."

The shadowy and rosy gloom of the room suddenly disappeared. The glinting fog vanished. I lay still for a moment, looking at the earthquake crack in the ceiling plaster, and saw the dust on the windowsill.

"You . . . sure . . . that's what you want?" I finally said, choking a little at the last.

"Yep," he said. Now he was grinning. "Allus works for me."

There's no memory of climbing aboard. But soon I felt my cock in a hot place, with a tongue swirling around the head of it, and lips moving up towards my pubic hair, with a suction powerfully drawing me down towards his face. I saw the dark red of his lips encircling the shaft, and between my legs felt his forearm move as he manipulated himself.

In a moment he pushed me out of his mouth. "I'm ready now for another go-'round," he said, laughing.

I put one foot on the floor beside the bed, and threw my other leg back over his body. "Well, I'm not," I said. "I'm pooped."

"Aw, c'mon. I got it nice and hard agin."

"Nope," I said, now standing beside the bed.

"Then blow me," he said, waggling his cock between his fingers.

"Not now," I said. My body was sweating, my armpits and crotch wet with secret tears.

"Then jack me off."

"Do it yourself," I said. "I'm gonna go wash."

In the bathroom I turned on the water and sat down. A delayed reaction set in. I started to tremble. I put my face against the washbowl briefly. The rim was cool.

Suddenly I knew exactly how the Firbank man in the Hilton had felt. The image had cracked, the dream had fled. I thought of the things Prospero had made me do, and remembered Poe: *The thousand injuries of Fortunato I had born as best I could, but when he ventured upon* . . . well, not "insult," nor did I vow revenge, but over my whole life, and especially over the past weeks with Prospero, a harsh and glaring light had fallen that made everything look dingy and absurdly real.

After a few moments I heard the springs creak as he got out of bed, then the soft sounds of him dressing, and finally I came out of the bathroom.

"Oh," he said, "what a helluva night."

"Yeah," I said, drying my hands on the towel which I kept carefully in front of me. The tile was cold under my feet.

"Well, t'anks, ole buddy," he said, extending his hand. "See you next week."

His hand was hot and firm. I shook it.

"Yeah," I said.

I never saw him again.

On Andros Island

Sometimes a whim will take you far—literally.

It all began with my strolling along the side of Union Square in San Francisco last summer. In the window of a travel agency a display caught my eye, and sent a shock down my spine. Amidst colorful photographs of underwater coral, great white beaches, and turquoise water was a lettered sign praising the beauties of the Bahamas, and among them a display saying "Visit Andros."

I'd known, of course, being of Greek heritage, that there was an island called Andros in the Aegean sea, known for its silks and wines and lemons. But I had no idea there was one in the Bahamas. And all of a sudden, the idea of an Andros visiting Andros seemed delightful for a number of reasons.

One was that I was enduring a kind of world-weariness with hustling that summer in San Francisco. My psyche felt soiled, snail-tracked with pearly trails of semen, discolored with old saliva and worse. And another reason was that it had been a cold summer. Someone once said that the coldest winter of his life had been a summer spent in San Francisco, and that year I felt inclined to agree. You couldn't go shirtless under just a leather jacket the way you could in Los Angeles, and you certainly couldn't go jacketless at all. It was turtleneck time, and that could rarely help a hustler's image.

So I was up and away. I packed a bag, grabbed my passport, closed my little house and turned on all the burglar alarms, spread the proper airplane's wings, and flew to Miami, and thence to

125

Nassau and from there to Andros Town. From there I went by taxi (wow! the price!) clear down to the south end of Andros Island. I stayed at Las Palmas Hotel, one of the resorts on the eastern shore.

I went to the rustic "office" to register. The heat was all around, against my body like a warm lover, and after the chill of California it was wonderful. The "hotel" was a cluster of low bungalows built around a large swimming pool overlooking a private beach. The colors and the sunshine already hurt my eyes, and I had to get out my dark glasses even before I looked at the sky and water. There were coconut palms growing tall in the garden.

"Would you like a standard or superior room?" the clerk inquired. There was a little sibilance in his voice—a giveaway. He was tanned to the appearance of rich Corinthian leather, and his skin looked dry and old. He must have been all of twenty-eight. The sun is a violent mistress in the tropics; she ages you before your time. I couldn't tell whether he was British or American.

"Superior," I said, going the whole hog.

I blinked a little when he told me the price, but what the hell. I gave him the passport. His reaction was the same as that of the airline clerk in Miami. "My god," he said. "Andros!"

"Yup," I said, grinning. "Thought I'd see how the old home island was getting along."

"By damn," he said. "You're the first Andros ever to come here."

"Except, of course, Sir Edmund, after whom the place was named," I said sardonically.

"You'll hardly need your leather jacket here," he said, equally sardonic. I'd taken it off and slung it across my shoulder, and was resplendent in white T-shirt, nipples showing. I looked at him. He was not a bad-lookin' dude—enough chest muscles, good pecs. His nose had been broken. His blond hair was bleached almost white.

"I can tell that already," I said. "The place is hot."

At that he cocked an eyebrow and gave me a careful lookover. "My name's Kenny," he said.

"And you know mine," I said. "Any action around here?"

"You makes your own," he said, after a moment. A slight smile. I pegged him for an American because of his accent. Faintly Floridian, I thought. Perhaps a club-member.

"Where you from?" I said, signing the registration form.

"Florida," he said, looking at the card. "Ah," he said. "Berkeley. I've been there."

And away we went. He'd been on Andros for six months. "What do you do?" he said.

I grinned. "Sex therapist and consultant," I said.

"I'll put you in cottage three," he said. "You'll like it. Good view of the beach and all that goes on. There aren't many guests here just now. About twenty. You make twenty-one."

"What are they like?"

"Congenial," he said. "Rich. But mostly older or married. They do a lot of diving. You dive?"

"Some scuba," I said.

"You'll like that. It's really beautiful underwater."

"Above water too, I see," I said. The half-moon beach stretched to eternity, white and glistening, and was lost in shades of blue water and the dark blue cloudless sky. I had a feeling I was going to enjoy the vacation.

The room was great—air-conditioned, no less, and decorated with deep-toned warm red and brown fabrics and bedcover; a bathroom was tiled in pale green, and a little patio baked in the sun outside the sliding glass doors. There were hangings and pillows here and there of what I was later to learn were called Androsian batiks, colorful tropical-looking things all right for the Bahamas, I reckoned, but looking half-savage and Californian, and perhaps a little too elegant for a hustler.

I spent the next two days getting acquainted with the other guests—stereotypes all. A British army officer and his lank-haired wife, both in their last half-centuries. An old-maid schoolteacher from Vermont. An elderly lush, who kept telling stories about World War II. The manager and his wife, fat and prosperous. They were all distinguished by leathery skins and dark tans, with white-etched wrinkles around their squinted eyes—especially the beachcomber bum who had arrived eight years previously and never left. The only exception was the schoolteacher from Vermont—who carried a parasol and didn't let her face get into the sun. All the others represented a dermatologist's dream a few years hence; if they didn't have skin troubles by now they would then.

And I did some scuba diving. That was really a treat, with the water almost tepid except where the barrier reef broke and what they called the "tongue of the ocean" came in—a deep drop-off, quite dangerous, with the water as you swam suddenly changing to ice. The coral grew in brilliant fields of green, rose, yellow, white—rainbow hues, quite visible inside the reef through crystalline water, and farther out deeper hued. When you were exploring the fronds waving on the sea-bottom, looking up you could see the shimmering silver of the underside of the wavelets like molten metal quivering. Beautiful.

I lay on the beach and in two days was almost black, my Greek skin producing the quick tan that I had always enjoyed. The second night I had a visitor. It was Kenny. He arrived while I was recovering from eating too much conch chowder, lobster, and hot Johnny bread. He had a bottle of Beefeater gin in hand.

"How's about a drink?" he said rather thickly. He'd obviously had several.

"Okay," I said, getting glasses and some ice from the small refrigerator.

"Damn," he said, half sprawling on one elbow on the bed, "you sure got dark in a hurry. All over?" he asked. "There's a fenced-off place where you can let it all hang out."

"No thanks," I said."I keep a contrast in the middle part, so's I can see how dark I am. It's sexier."

"You're one sexy dude," he said. And then, with a wisdom he may have got as a hotel clerk he said, "You a hustler?"

I waggled my hand at him. "Have been," I said. "I'm on vacation now."

"Aw," he said. "I wanna get fucked. Tell you what. I ain't got the dough, but I'll fix it so you can have an extra night and day free."

I didn't much feel like it, but then there had been times like that before. "All right," I said, and pulled off my white T-shirt. He ran his tongue over his upper lip. "Damn," he said, "you sure got a well-developed body. You work out?"

"Fucking," I said. "It's good for the back and shoulders. Helps the arms and legs too." I took the drink he'd poured and gulped half of it. The gin was fine and aromatic. It burned a hot little path down my throat and into my stomach where it got lost.

"Okay, baby," I said, swatting the bed and then unfastening my belt and zipper. "Let's get goin'." I picked up the small jar of cold

128

cream I always carried and hefted it in my hand. Then I took off my chinos and the zoris I had been wearing everywhere. Life was very informal on Andros Island.

He stood up a little drunkenly and undressed, almost losing his balance as he tried to raise one leg to get out of his slacks. "Guess I'm a little drunkee," he said, almost giggling. He had a sort of lean ropy body with no tan line at all. His dingdong was hard and fairly sizable. There was blond hair everywhere, thick on his legs. The one light in the room made him glow a little around the edges.

"How you want it?" I asked, laying a hand on ole Betsy and giving her a coupla strokes.

"Lemme bend over the bed," he said, "while you stand. But say," he said, "fix the mirror in the bathroom door, will yuh?"

"Fix it how?"

"So's it focuses on the bed," he said. "I wanta watch you."

It'd be nice to watch myself too, I thought, and angled the door. "How's that?"

" 'Bout an inch more," he said, from his bent position on the bed. "There."

I returned to the bed with a towel. I laid a fingerful of cream against the crack in front of me and then approached. At the first touch he jumped a little.

"Take it easy," he said. "I ain't been screwed in quite a while. And you're big."

I felt the first warm touch of his hole against the head of my cock, and the little coolness from the not quite melted grease. And then my reflexes took over, and my dreams began. I half shut my eyes, cutting out the sight of the whole room and his body, all except the dark tanned crack before me, and the darker hair around the celestial gate. Slowly, little by little, I eased the head in—felt the strong barrier of his sphincter, stopped for a moment, and then with a dozen small jolts pressed onward. Glancing down I watched the thick column of my cock, shining in the dim light, as it slowly worked inward, ever inward, until my groin was pressed tight against his heated flesh, and then withdrew just as leisurely, watching the glistening shaft appear again and slowly lengthen until I felt it almost withdrawn, and then another slow push inward.

He had commenced a low keening, almost a moan, in which I

129

could now and again hear whispered words of "Fuck me, oh fuck me, fuck," over and over, a soft litany of begging and pleading, and then taking on a different tone from the pleasure he must have been feeling — and I spread my legs and bent my knees, liking it as much as he seemed to, aware of the clutching hotness of that tunnel pressing against my cock from all sides, enfolding me like warm hands grasping, like a warm glove fitted over me. Little by little my eyelids went entirely shut, pressed hard together until green and red lights swam against the blackness of my lids, and soldiers and sailors and cops swarmed over me, and I licked their boots and feet, and felt their hands upon me, dozens and dozens of them, reaching, grasping. My flesh tightened all over my body, and the tiny fire-flowers began to swim out of the darkness, to dance on my shoulders and my moving hips, and suddenly with a great flare to explode within me, drawing all my feeling to my cock and holding it there in the intolerable whirlwind of the orgasm that rushed over and through me. At the same time I felt the extraordinary clamping of his own coming, and his muscles swept up and down the length of my cock. I collapsed on top of him, my hand reaching under him, and finding his palm wet with his own gyzym.

So we lay for a long moment, the sweat running down my ribs from my armpits and cooling as it fell on his skin. Finally he struggled a bit, and slowly I withdrew, waiting for the great words from him, the poetry that would be memorable in my mind forever.

"Goddlemighty," he said. "That was dandy."

The next afternoon I put on my skimpiest briefs, the black ones, and went exploring, walking down along the great half-moon curve of white and glittering sand towards the land's end. Andros was a low-lying island, cut across with water and inlets leading far back into the dense tropical forest that Ken told me had never been fully explored. The native huts were down the other way — well, not huts really, but small houses sturdily built of native limestone and coral to withstand the hurricanes that came sweeping down out of the storm womb of the Caribbean. It was rugged bush and mangrove country, and years ago had harbored countless thousands of flamingos until the young low-flying sprouts of airmen, training during World War II, had scared 'em all off.

130

But I was here to restore my psyche, not do a piece for the *National Geographic*. I walked barefoot in the warm and sensual sand and watched the curling waves, and felt the sun lustfully on my body. I went about two miles, looked back and saw no one, and took off my skimpy briefs and lay down on the hot sand.

It was utterly still, save for the gentle sound of the low waves, and the cry of an occasional bird far-off in the forest that edged the beach. I had enough sense, even though lulled into drowsiness by sun and breeze and surf, to put my towel over my crotch to keep from burning the father of all evil, lying lengthy down my leg.

I lay with closed eyes, almost asleep, when suddenly I heard a strange sound coming from the ocean, or seeming to—above the curling gentle swish of the waves there was added the sound almost of someone walking, or of some differing sound of the waves. I opened my eyes to look.

It was a man, rising from the sea, raising each foot and plunging it straight down into the water. He was about twenty feet away, and not looking in my direction at all. My ole Greek brain, nurtured on mythology and thinking back to my ancestral roots, could not remember any romantic hero who had risen from the foam—not Apollo nor Adonis, and certainly he did not remind me of Venus rising, for he was naked, and the pendulous thing that swung lazily from side to side, faintly slapping against each leg as he walked, might well have been the envy of Venus, but was certainly not her own. He seemed young, maybe early twenties.

I was suddenly, violently, and irreversibly in love . . . or lust. I don't know what it was about him, what allure or attraction or magnetism, but I was immediately hooked. He was not exceedingly tall, perhaps not even as tall as I was, but everything about him seemed perfect. The face was molded in a classic pattern— broad clear untroubled forehead, straight black eyebrows that dipped downwards to his cheekbones at the far ends, a straight nose above sensually curved and carved lips, deep-red and shining from the sea-water. The body itself might have been the model for Leonardo's sketch of the perfectly proportioned man, that figure in the circle with arms extended. It was a body that Michelangelo might have laid down his chisel and stepped back to admire. The shoulders were broad, the pectorals swelling with strength, and

131

the forearms darkened with the black hair on them, now wet and flowing in one direction. As more of his body appeared above the silvered water, I saw the hair on his legs running in the same direction, almost as if he wore a ribbed and patterned garment. Magnetism . . . the air around him almost crackled with electricity and sex . . .

He raised a hand and smiled, heading towards me.

"Hullo," he said, smiling still more widely. Unconsciously I pulled the towel over my crotch into a modest placement. "My name's Andy." He extended his hand.

I reached up from the sand and took it. "Phil Andros," I said. His grip was strong.

"Oh," he said. "You're the fellow Ken told me about. I got in late last night, and Ken was talking about your last name. He said that by now the whole island knows about it. Even the natives. One of them said you were the great white god and father, come home at last."

There was nothing to do but laugh. "I had no idea it'd cause so much talk," I said, and then, "you're British, aren't you?"

"Yes," he said. Oh lord, those white white teeth!

"You've been here before?" I said, a half-question.

"Oh yes, three or four times. I like it very much. Quiet, serene. Gives you a good chance to get away from the world and still be in it, in a manner of speaking."

He looked out towards the limitless ocean, and then lay down beside me. "You don't mind?" he said with a smile.

"Not at all," I said, falling into a kind of phony British speech pattern. It's always like that. Let me be around an Englishman, a Frenchman, or whatever, and within minutes I'm almost parodying the speech I hear. I couldn't take my eyes away from his face. The dreams that my mind was creating were beginning to be reflected in ole Betsy under the towel.

He sighed deeply and lay back on the sand. "Thank God there aren't any girls around at the moment," he said.

I didn't know exactly how to take that—whether he was glad since we were both comfortably naked, or what.

"They give you much trouble?" I asked.

"Sometimes," he said. "Do they you?"

"Not at all," I said.

"Ken said you were a sex therapist."

I stuck my tongue-point into my cheek. "I'm good at reducing swellings of all kinds . . . the brain . . . and other things."

He laughed a little, took sand in his hand, and let it slide out the bottom. "I guess I'm bisexual," he said.

"Not unusual," I said, running my tongue over my lips which had gone extremely dry.

"It's been quite a while since I went to bed with a chap," he said. "Would you feel like trying it, after dinner?"

A skyrocket must have gone off somewhere in one of the valleys of my brain. "Oh sure," I said. "There's not much to do around here in the evenings." Things were happening a little fast even for me.

"What do you do?" I asked.

He looked at me oddly.

"I mean," I said, "what's your line of work?"

"I just live," he said, smiling.

"In London?" He nodded. "Whereabouts?"

He shrugged. "Several places," he said.

Ah, he was rich, then. We talked a little more, about nothing in particular, and then we headed back towards the cottages. He had the one next to mine — cottage four.

I was in a daze when I closed the door and made for the shower. What in the hell was happening to me? I could count on the fingers of one hand the number of times I'd really felt a deep affection . . . love, perhaps, for anyone: Kenny, the farm boy from downstate Illinois, Greg Wolfson, the cop in San Francisco, two or three others. But this one had me dizzy. This was either infatuation or a real obsession. And in the midst of it I felt the little nagging certainty that I'd seen this cat before — maybe one of those anonymous faces you see on a movie screen in a crowd, so perfect, so handsome, that it takes your breath — and of course you never learn who it is, nor see him again. I had pretty well held the reins on my feelings for many years, knowing better than to get involved . . . hustlers just couldn't afford that. It was ruinous . . . Time enough when you were forty to find a companion and settle down — if you could find anyone who'd have you at that age.

After the shower I lay down on the bed, naked, and ran my hand over my chest hair. He had a charming little sprinkling on his chest, which added rather than detracted. I looked down at my body, now thirty-three, and decided it was not too bad. The belly was even sunken — but then, remembering that I was lying down, I stood up again to survey myself in the mirror. Not bad — but my face looked a little tougher, and my nipples turned down; they were still large, but the angle had changed. The feet were fine, and the calves, and there was hair on the toe-knuckles, and the second toe longer than the big toe, as it was on classic statues. Thighs were okay too, and ole Betsy still arced out. Sidewise, the butt still looked good, the pectorals firm, and the upper arms bigger than ever. And the skin was smooth; I slid my hand over my torso, and was not unpleased.

He was going to come in an hour, he said, and bring a bottle of gin. Gin helped a lot. I lay back on the bed and thought about him. Outside was the soft murmuring sound of the surf, and a vagrant breeze wandered through the room. Romance under the moon and stars, by gum — for the first time in years and years. I pictured his body again — every tendon, every muscle, every swelling and hollow — in neck, in throat, on chest, thighs, and legs — even his armpits were perfect. I wanted to bury my mouth in them. And yet does not a lovesick guy see no fault whatever in his beloved? My cynicism told me that in a few weeks I would not like the way he tapped his cigarette, nor pulled on his socks, nor stood shaving. Yet here I was — fantasizing a whole life with him when I knew that I might be lucky if I could spend an entire night in his company.

There was a knock on the door, rather tentative. It was Andy, grinning from here to there, and holding a bottle of Boodle's gin by the neck. He had on a maroon bathrobe, which he took off at once, standing as naked as I was.

"Am I early?" he asked in his husky baritone.

"As a matter of fact, you're late. My nails are chewed down to the nubbin."

"I'll bet," he said, sardonic.

"Just a minute, bub," I said. "Before anything begins, I'd really like to know where I've seen you before."

"I've a very common face," he said. Adonis stood before me.

"That's not exactly true," I said, folding my arms. "I *know* I've seen you."

134

He was silent for a very long time. Then he said, "If I tell you, will you not say anything to anyone?"

"Cross my heart," I said, doing it.

He cleared his throat. "You may have seen me on the deck of the *Intrepid*," he said slowly.

Baffled, I said, "A sailor?"

"Royal Naval Air," he said.

I still didn't get it. "I watched the Falklands episode a lot," I said.

"Or perhaps you saw me at the right of the altar. At the wedding." A long pause. "Of Prince Charles."

The pores rose all over my body. The lust I felt for him had made ole Betsy rise, but the jolt of his revelation took it all away. Shocked, I sat down on the bed, flabber and gasted. A meteor hit me, and the illumination was blinding. I looked at him carefully, the black hair combed neat and straight, the generous mouth, the eyebrows, the full red lips, the beautiful body. Oddly, my eyes concentrated on the patch of chest hair, unable to move from his chest. "Andy," I said. My mouth was very dry. "Andrew. The royal family."

He shrugged.

"Goddlemighty," I said. "Randy Andy. Everyone knows about you."

He shrugged again. "I come down here incognito two or three times a year, if I can." He looked at me. "Please don't tell anybody."

I shook my head. "Of course not. Hustlers never do."

I knelt in front of him. He put his strong hands gently on the top of my head, and then slipped one of them down to my neck. I took his cock into my mouth, using all the Kama Sutra tricks I knew, the nibbling, the interior suction, the kissing and the licking down the shaft, the swirling around the glans, the tongue into the meatus, all, all of the devices I had learned in all the years of hustling. I pushed him back on the bed and gave him a partial tongue bath, sucking all of his toes, figure-eighting them, and getting the two big toes into my mouth at the same time. A frenzy was on me. And finally he—tossing and turning and moaning a little—put his hand gently against my back and turned me over. There was a fumbling at the drawer of the nightstand, and then I felt the coolness of the grease applied, and heard the soft sliding sound as he rubbed it the length of his cock. Then supine, conquered, fucked

135

by a princeling, I lay quiet. He kneeled between my outspread legs and guided it in, first a little, thence to more. He was both gentle and aggressive. I had to bite my lip a couple of times, and my back was sweating. I didn't care. It was grand.

At last his thrusts grew faster, and my hips rose to meet his deep strokes. He knew how to fuck, and he hit my joyspot every time, sending me reeling into Never-Never Land where I fell down a rabbit hole, ate the magic mushroom, and grew a monstrous cock. Fantasies of knights in armor fled through my tightly closed eyelids; novas and galaxies exploded, were born and flared and died—and I came all over the Androsian batik. I felt him shoot almost at the same time, his cock expanding and contracting with each spurt.

And then we rested quietly sweating belly to back, while we crawled back up out of the "little death," as the French call it.

"Andy," I said, "Prince or not, I'm gonna kiss you," and I pulled his head down, with my hand behind his neck. His mouth opened, and for about three minutes our tongues fought duels, little battles with no one winning, and then subsiding into a gentle caressing, warm and passion-filled.

Finally we broke loose. "My word," said Andrew. "I think you must be the best there is. The next time I come to the States, I hope I'll see you. Or maybe meet you here on Andros. Will you give me your address?"

I did, and he gave me his, which was a box number in London.

"I have to leave tomorrow morning early," he said.

"Oh god," I said. I kneeled before him. "But not before I give you homage." I put my cheek against his pubic hair and licked it with my tongue. "My liege," I murmured, a knight before his sovereign.

God, what a romantic I was.

He pulled me to my feet and put his well-formed arms around me. "We'll see each other again," he said. "I promise."

"I hope so," I said.

The next morning about nine I went to the desk.

"Has Andy gone?" I asked Ken.

"At five this morning," he said. "Didn't you hear the helicopter?"

"No," I said. "I had no idea he was a prince. Randy Andy."

"He's not," said Ken, shortly. "He's a look-alike. The family hires him to stand in for Prince Andrew. But his name really is Andrew Windsor. He also makes a bundle modeling—clothes on Saville Row and all that. But I think the royal family's gonna pull his cork. He's about to get sued, or rather his sponsors are. The family doesn't want his face on tea-biscuit tins all over England."

My face must have been scarlet, but I smiled. "Oh, well," I said, "if he's fired he can always get a job in New York. They're not so fussy, and they'd be proud to have a handsome look-alike stud as a model."

"I had him once," Ken said. "He's very picky. You were lucky to have had him last night. I tried several times to get his address but I couldn't. Very private person."

"Well, I got it," I said. "It takes more than luck, I guess."

"Such as what?" said Ken, very irritated.

I grinned my friendliest at him, and grabbed my cock through my pants.

"This'll do it," I said, and left the room, momentarily angry. But then I reconsidered. Maybe Ken had been lying, maybe not. After all, it had been a fine fuck, and perhaps if he were really telling the truth—that it wasn't the prince—it might turn out to be the closest I would ever come to getting royally screwed.

Ecco Narcissus!

Like long-stemmed black tulips, the motorcyclists gather in Doc's Place, and when the room is warm and filled, the smell of their leather is strong and exciting in the heavy air—their black jackets, their great heavy gloves, their thick black leather trousers. After they arrive it is much too late for a "civilian" to enter; you must be there before they come.

And I was, and already drunk. A little luminous haze, opalescent, arose from my drink; it floated out into the room; my eyes hardly focused. The air was thick with the bittersweet muskiness of warm leather. The barstool revolved like a slow carousel; faces drifted past, and bodies rose tenuously from the floor, long black legs, shining buckles, gleaming visors—like a surrealist dream, like a hashish nightmare—sparklets of light, noise from a rainbowed jukebox, jostling of the elbows, nudging of a rib, a hand on an arm, a leather kneecap grown large and roomfilling—oh, I was drunk!

A tall black figure swam into view, his eyes (no—they were goggles!) pushed back on his tight crash helmet. He gripped my arms. "I'll see you home," he said. "No," said he, "we'll walk, not ride."

The nip of autumn air, the sidewalks—where to? Where to? We found the apartment, and then it was his turn. He opened the bottles, he sampled them all. I fell into bed, whilst he went to the bathroom, my bathroom with the rosy lights, the walls of tall mirrors, triangulated to show you all, your back, your front, your sides, everyting—all at once, too much. A thousand of you run away into the distance, a thousand persons move their fingers as you do, and off in the dim and rosy dusk the darkened shadows of faraway bodies crouch to watch you.

The slow maelstrom of my bed received me, the vortex turned slowly around; lights winked, colors came and went, there was silent music crashing (now loud, now pianissimo) in my secret ear. And turning, turning, the bed bore me in a circle around the square limits of the room.

"Come to bed!" I rose half upright and shouted. "In a minute," he called. I stumbled to the door of the bathroom, peeked through the crack. He stood naked, one hand caressing the shoulder and arm of his other side. Over and over again, while he watched in the mirrors a thousand tall and ivory figures stroking their arms, their thighs, the flatness of their bellies, posing, turning, the faces in profile, in full—the rosy lights catching and weaving a pattern of light and shadow, beautiful, beautiful . . .

I reeled to bed again, and the slow circular turning bore me down, down, and red poppies filled the air with slumbrous fragrance, and there was a note struck like a crystal bell.

Then it was dawn. Through the black curtains sliced a thin edge of chill grey light. I listened and moved my tongue over dry lips. The rosy lights were still on, and I heard the faint sound of rustling, of stroking . . . I staggered to the crack of the door and looked.

The window was a little open, a vagrant breeze filtered through. It rustled the green leaves of a gigantic flower, rooted in the mosaic of the floor—ceiling tall, the green stem slender and swaying, and the white calyx bent down. The sweet odor overpowered me. "Tom!" I called, opening the door.

Nothing, nothing—only the thin rustle of the pointed leaves caressing the stem, the whisper of the white flowers turning ever so slightly, paper-thin, funereal sweet. And in the silent mirrors, a thousand milk-white narcissi bowed a little.

Oh, I am the envy of my friends! Now they come very night to visit me, to see my wondrous bloom! So little trouble—a bit of water once a day! The scent—as of heaven sprinkled in the room!

And I, so happy with my flower, tending it, loving it (the hunting days are ended), caressing its stem, plucking its petals, inhaling

139

the terrible odor of its chalice, and (a secret!) oft-times at night feeling it slip into my room, to wind its tendrils gently around my body, pinioning my arms to my sides, fastening my legs to the bed—almost like wide webbed straps, while I lie in the gentle embrace of my flower, knowing it cannot escape, for I hold it and it holds me, and the wide window has grown bars of itself, so that my Tom can never leave.

Other Grey Fox books of interest: